P9-EFI-567

McBAIN DUET

McBAIN DUET

Driving Lessons and *Petals*

Two Novellas

by

Ed McBain

With a special introduction
by the author

Mystery Guild
Garden City, New York

Driving Lessons

First Carroll & Graf edition 2000

Carroll & Graf Publishers, Inc.
A Division of Avalon Publishing
19 West 21st Street
New York, NY 10010-6805

Petals

ISBN 0-7394-1535-2

Manufactured in the United States of America

This, yet again, time, is for my wife—

DRAGICA DIMITRIJEVIĆ-HUNTER

DUET INTRODUCTION

Once upon a time, while I was doing research for an Evan Hunter novel titled STREETS OF GOLD, the pianist John Mehegan told me that a good jazz musician should be able to play any tune in all twelve keys. I've always believed the same thing about writing.

If a writer knew what he was doing, he should be able to write anything. He should be able to crawl into the skin of a male murderer in Manhattan or a female librarian in Dubuque, Iowa, he should know how to become—yes, *become*—a computer nerd or a football hero, a Martian or a Masai warrior, a prima ballerina or a truck driver hauling lumber cross-country in the empty hours of the night.

When I was learning to write crime fiction, I tried all the sub-genres: Woman in Jeopardy, Man on the Run, Innocent Bystander, Amateur Detective, Private Eye, and—at long last—what has now come to be called the Police Procedural. But even though novels about cops have occupied most of my writing time since 1956, every now and then I'll take a break from those hard-working men and women of the Eight-Seven; life in the big bad city can be cruel and often unjust, you know, so it's important to seek greener pastures once in a while. The irony is that wherever I may roam—as Ed McBain, anyway—I always seem to stumble over a corpse or two.

I wrote PETALS because I was fascinated by what John Le Carré was doing with the spy novel. I knew he'd once worked with British intelligence, but it seemed to me that the novels he based upon that experience were much richer and more inventive than anything the experience could have promised. In 1956, I'd taken hours of research and molded them into my own vision of what police work should look like, creating a fictitious world called CopLand, if you will. Now, starting in 1963, Le Carré was using his own experience to create a landscape that for him—and for me and millions of other grateful readers—became simply SpyLand.

A good jazz musician should be able to play any tune in all twelve keys.

SpyLand was a tune I'd never played in any key.

While writing it, all I tried to do (within the framework of a highly suspenseful story, I hope) was recreate the same sense of reality that exists (again, I *hope*) in the 87th Precinct novels—what one of my editors once called "clinical verity." I had long since learned that if any single element in a realistic tale seemed false or contrived, the entire house of cards would collapse. I tried very hard to make everything in PETALS seem as real as Tuesday.

In much the same way, DRIVING LESSONS, was a detour from the Eight-Seven. The setting here, like that of the fictitious city in the 87th Precinct novels, is imaginary. But this is a place of forests and streams, and towns named Lake Paskonomee and River Close, with populations that could fit into any small corner of Isola. In the small town that embraces this story, the cop shop is called "Raleigh Station" instead of "87th Precinct," and the "District Attorney" is a "State Attorney." Here in River Close, until the relatively recent formation of a detective division, any big case required calling in detectives from the county seat "up Twin River Junction." We are very far from the mean streets of Isola here. We are, in fact, deep in America's heartland.

Katie Logan is the detective in this story.

There have been female detectives in the 87th Precinct novels, and I have often related large sections of any given mystery from their viewpoint. But this is the first time I've written a mystery from an almost exclusively female viewpoint, and this too is a departure. Once upon a time—when you and I were young, Maggie—a woman critic for an important newspaper said that I didn't know how to write women. My women were only sex objects. My women were stick figures. My women were appalling. Oh yeah? I thought. *Yeah,* she thought.

So I deliberately sat down to write a novel from the viewpoints of three generations of American women—a grandmother, a mother, and a daughter. I interviewed scores of women, and I studied books about the feminine psyche and the mysteries of romantic yearnings and manly ambitions and menstruation and the tedium of housework and child-raising, and the glory of having hair that fell to the middle of the back. And finally I wrote the chapter I knew would either take me over the top forever or else land me flat on my back in the gutter. I wrote about giving birth. From the viewpoint of the woman having the baby. That was in an Evan Hunter novel titled MOTHERS AND DAUGHTERS, published in 1960. I've never worried about writing real women again.

So here's DUET.

A spy story—huh?—together with a cop story set in a small town—huh again?—by the same guy who writes those big-city novels about the 87th Precinct? Yep. Same guy sitting side by side with himself at opposite ends of the piano, playing two different tunes in two different keys. It's not quite the same recital that Evan Hunter and Ed McBain perform in CANDYLAND, where two *different* guys are playing the same tune in their own distinct styles, but it's all jazz, man, and maybe it's even good jazz.

ED McBAIN

McBAIN DUET

DRIVING LESSONS

The girl looked sixteen and blonde, and the man looked thirty-two and dazed. The responding blues were questioning the girl and trying to question the man who'd been in the vehicle. They weren't expecting much from the man, not in his condition.

They thought at first he was drunk even though he didn't smell of alcohol. The girl was cold sober. Hysterical because she'd just run somebody over, but cold sober nonetheless. She was the one who'd been driving the car.

"What's your name, miss?" one of the blues asked.

"Rebecca Patton. Is she all right?"

"May I see your license, please?"

"I don't have a license. I'm just learning to drive. I have a learner's permit. Is the woman all right?"

"May I see the permit, please?"

The officer should have known, but didn't, that in this state, within many sections of the Vehicle and Traffic Law, a learner's permit was deemed a license to drive. All he knew was that here was a sobbing sixteen-year-old kid who'd just run over a woman who looked like she was maybe twenty-eight, twenty-nine years old.

They were standing outside the vehicle that had knocked her down, a blue Ford Escort with dual brake pedals and oversized yellow and black STUDENT DRIVER plates on the front and rear bumpers. The impact had sent the woman flying some five feet into the air, tossing her onto a pile of burning leaves stacked on the sidewalk near the curb. One of the witnesses had dragged her off the smoldering fire, onto the lawn, and had immediately called the police. Other blues at the scene were still searching for the handbag the witness said she'd been carrying. But the stricken woman was wearing red, and the leaves on the ground were thick this fall.

They kept scuffing through the fallen leaves, searching for the camouflaged bag, hoping to find a driver's license, a business card, a phone bill with a name and address on it—anything that would tell them who she was. Anonymous, she lay in the gutter some twenty feet from where a highway patrol car was just pulling in behind the Ford. Red coat open over a blue skirt and jacket, white blouse with a stock tie. Eyes closed. Hands at her sides, palms upward, fingers twitching.

The blues took the highway patrolmen aside and informed them that they'd tested the guy's skills and he'd failed with flying colors and seemed to be high on something. Nobody smelt alcohol but they gave him a breathalyzer test, anyway, and discovered no trace whatever of methyl alcohol in his system, the guy blew much lower than point-one-oh. One of them asked him his name, which the blues had already done. He still didn't know. Shook his head and almost fell off his feet. They opened the door on the passenger side of the Ford and let him sit.

"He's Mr. Newell," the girl said. "He's been giving me driving lessons. I don't know how this happened, she just stepped off the curb. Oh my God, is she all right?"

"Can you tell us his first name?"

"Andrew. Will she be all right?"

The ambulance arrived along about then. It was almost three thirty. Paramedics lifted the woman onto a stretcher and hoisted her inside. The ambulance pulled away from the curb. Nobody yet knew who the woman was. The street seemed suddenly very still. A fresh wind sent withering leaves rattling along the curb.

"I think you'll both have to come along with us," one of the blues said to the young blonde girl and the man who seemed stoned.

The girl nodded.

"Will you call my father, please?" she asked.

The phone was ringing when Katie got back to the apartment that afternoon. She put the two bags of groceries on the table just inside the door and went swiftly to the kitchen counter, sitting on one of the stools there and yanking the phone from its wall hook at the same time.

"Logan," she said.

"Katie, it's Carl."

"Yes, Carl."

"Can you get down here right away? Lieutenant needs you to question a female juve."

"Sure," she said. "Give me ten minutes."

"See you," Carl said, and hung up.

Katie sighed and put the phone back on its hook. This was supposed to be her day off. But she was the only woman detective in the department and whenever they got a young girl in, the job went to her. She was wearing, on this bright fall afternoon, a tan plaid skirt with low heels, opaque brown pantyhose and a matching brown sweater. The skirt was on the short side; she'd have to change before driving downtown. She'd also have to call Max again to see if there was any further word from her dear departed husband. Worst thing about a detective squadroom in a small town was the lack of privacy. River Close claimed a mere 50,000 inhabitants—well, some fifty-five during July and August, but all the summer renters were gone now.

She went to the kitchen window and cranked it open. A gust of cool air rushed into the apartment, carrying with it the aroma of woodsmoke. From the junior high school across the street, she could hear the sounds of football practice. Today was the sixteenth of October, a clear brisk day during one of the most glorious falls Katie could recall. Spoiled, of course. Autumn spoiled forever. Stephen had left her on the twelfth of September. Easy come, easy go, she thought. She'd only known him since she was sixteen.

Until now, she'd always thought of autumn as her time of year. Sometimes felt she even *looked* like autumn, the reddish-brown hair and freckled cheeks echoing the season's colors, her eyes as blue as any September sky. She'd hated the freckles when she was a little girl, but at thirty-three she felt they added character to her face. Made her look a bit more Irish, too, as if she needed any help with a name like Katherine Byrne Logan.

She wondered all at once if she should go back to her maiden name after the divorce. She was so used to being Katie Logan, so used to being Detective Logan, so used to being just plain *Logan* that . . .

Call Max, she thought.

She looked at the wall clock. Ten minutes to four. Better get cracking.

First the frozen stuff, she thought, and began unpacking the groceries.

Max Binder had been recommended to Katie by a lawyer she knew in the State Attorney's Office. A portly, avuncular man with white hair and chubby cheeks, he seemed uncommonly well-suited to the task of consoling forlorn women seeking divorces. Katie supposed she fell into this category. A forlorn woman. Deserted, desolate and forsaken. If she were any more Irish, she'd be keening. Instead, she was dialing the three B's and hoping Max wasn't in court.

"Binder, Benson and Byrd," said a woman's voice.

"Ellie, it's Katie Logan," she said. "Is he in?"

"Second."

Max came on the phone a moment later.

"Hi, Katie, what's new?" he asked.

Same question every time. What's new is my husband left me and is living with a twenty-two-year-old waitress is what's new.

"Have you heard from him?" she asked.

"Not yet."

"What's taking him so long?"

"He only got our counter-proposal a week ago. You're being eminently fair, Katie. I can't imagine him refusing at this point."

"Then call Schiffman and light a fire under him."

"Schiffman's trying a big case this week."

"Shall I call him myself?"

"Schiffman? No, no. No. No, Katie."

"How about Stephen then? My alleged husband."

"No. Certainly not."

"I want a divorce, Max."

"Of course you do. But be patient just a little longer, Katie. Please. I'm handling it. Please."

"OK, Max."

"OK, Katie? Please."

"Sure," she said. "Let me know."

She hung up and looked at the clock.

"On my way," she said aloud.

Rebecca Patton's dark-brown eyes were shining with tears. Behind her, the high windows of the room framed trees bursting with leaves of red, orange, yellow and brown. They were sitting in what the local precinct had labeled the "interrogation room", after those in big-city police departments, though normally the cops at Raleigh Station didn't put on airs. Katie hadn't yet told her that the woman she'd hit was in a critical condition at Gardner General Hospital. She hadn't yet told her that so far the woman hadn't been able to speak to anyone. Still anonymous, the hospital had admitted her as Jane Doe.

"Rebecca," Katie said, "your father just got here. If you'd like him to come in while we talk . . ."

"Yes, I would, please," Rebecca said.

"And if your mother would like to join us . . ."

"My mother's in California."

A sudden sharpness of voice which startled Katie.

"They're divorced."

"I see."

"I hope no one called her."

"I really don't know. I'm assuming the—"

She almost said "arresting officers".

She caught herself.

"—responding officers called whoever . . ."

"I didn't give them her name. I don't want her to know about this."

"If that's your wish."

"It's my wish."

"Let me get your father, then."

Dr. Ralph Patton was sitting on a bench in the corridor just outside the squadroom. He got to his feet the moment he saw Katie approaching. A tall spare man wearing blue jeans, a denim shirt, loafers and a suede vest, he looked more like a wrangler than a physician—but Wednesday was his day off. His dark-brown eyes were the color of his daughter's. They checked out the ID tag clipped to the pocket of Katie's gray tailored suit, and immediately clouded with suspicion.

"Where's Rebecca?" he asked.

"Waiting for us," Katie said. "She's fine, would you come with me, please?"

"What's she doing in a police station?"

"I thought you'd been informed . . ."

"Yes, the officer who called told me Rebecca was involved in an automobile accident. I repeat. What's she doing here?"

"Well, there are questions we have to ask, Dr. Patton, I'm sure you realize that. About the incident."

"Why? Since when is an accident a crime?"

"We haven't charged her with any crime," Katie said.

Which was true.

But a young woman lay critically injured in the hospital, knocked down by the automobile Rebecca Patton had been driving. And the only licensed driver in the subject vehicle had been under the influence of something, they still didn't know what. If the woman died, Katie figured Andrew Newell was looking at either vehicular homicide or reckless manslaughter. But whereas the law considered the licensed driver to be primary, if the learner behind the wheel *knew* that he wasn't in complete control of all his faculties, they might *both* be culpable.

"Are we going to need a lawyer here?" Dr. Patton asked, brown eyes narrowing suspiciously again.

"That's entirely up to you," Katie said.

"Yes, I want one," he said.

Technically, the girl was in police custody.

And in keeping with the guidelines, as a juvenile she was being questioned separately and apart from any criminals who might be on the premises, of whom there were none, at the moment, unless Andrew Newell in the lieutenant's office down the hall could be considered a criminal for having abused whatever substance was in his body when he'd climbed into that Ford.

The Patton lawyer was here now, straight out of Charles Dickens, wearing mutton chops and a tweedy jacket and a bow tie and gold-rimmed spectacles and sporting a checkered vest and a little pot belly and calling himself Alexander Wickett.

"How long have you been driving?" Katie asked.

"Since the beginning of August," Rebecca said.

"Does she have to answer these questions?" her father asked.

Wickett cleared his throat and looked startled.

"Why, no," he said. "Not if she doesn't wish to. You heard Miss Logan repeating Miranda in my presence."

"Then why don't you advise her to remain silent?"

"Well, do you *wish* to remain silent, Miss Patton?"

"Did I hurt that woman?" Rebecca asked.

"Yes, you hurt her," Katie said. "Very badly."

"Oh God."

"She's in critical condition at Gardner General."

"God, dear God."

"Do you want to answer questions or don't you?" Dr. Patton said.

"I want to help."

"Answering questions won't—"

"However I can help, I want to. I didn't mean to hit her. She stepped right off the curb. There was no way I could avoid her. I saw this flash of red and . . . and . . ."

"Becky, I think you should—"

"No. I want to help. Please." She turned to Katie and said, "Ask whatever you like, Miss Logan."

Katie nodded.

"Do you consider yourself a good driver, Rebecca?"

"Yes. I was planning to take my test next week, in fact."

"How fast were you going at the time of the accident?"

"Thirty miles an hour. That's the speed limit in that area."

"You've been there before?"

"Yes. Many times. We drive all over the city. Main roads, back roads, all over. Mr. Newell's a very good teacher. He exposes his students to all sorts of conditions. His theory is that good driving is knowing how to react instantly to any given circumstance."

"So you've been on that street before?"

"Yes."

"When did you first see the woman?"

"I told you. She stepped off the curb just as I was approaching the corner."

"Did you slow down at the corner?"

"No. There are full stop signs on the cross street. Both sides of Grove. But Third is the through street. I wasn't supposed to slow down."

"Did Mr. Newell advise you to use caution at that particular corner?"

"No. Why would he?"

"Did *he* see the woman before you did?"

"I don't think so."

"Well, did he say anything in warning?"

"No. What his system is, he asks his students to tell him everything they see. He'll say, 'What do you see?' And you'll answer, 'A milk truck pulling in,' or 'A girl on a bike,' or 'A red light,' or 'A car passing on my left,' like that. He doesn't comment unless you *don't* see something. Then he'll say again, 'What do you see *now*?' Emphasizing it. This way he knows everything going through our heads."

"When you approached that corner, did he ask you what you were seeing?"

"No. In fact, he'd been very quiet. I thought I must have been driving exceptionally well. But it was a pretty quiet afternoon, anyway. No video games."

"No what?"

"Video games. That's what he called unexpected situations. When everything erupts as if you're driving one of those cars in a video arcade? Six nuns on bicycles, a truck spinning out of control, a drunk staggering across the road. Video games."

"Did you at any time suspect that Mr. *Newell* might be drunk? Or under the influence of drugs?"

"Not until he got out of the car. After the accident."

"What happened then?"

"Well, first off, he almost fell down. He grabbed the car for support and then started to walk towards the police officer, but he was weaving and . . . and stumbling . . . acting just like a drunk, you know, but I knew he couldn't be drunk."

"How'd you know that?"

"Well, he wasn't drunk when we started the lesson, and he didn't have anything to drink while we were driving, so how could he be drunk?"

"But he couldn't even give the police his name, isn't that right?"

"Well, he could hardly talk at all. Just . . . you know . . . his speech was slurred, you could hardly understand him."

"Was this the case while you were driving? During the lesson?"

"No."

"He spoke clearly during the lesson?"

"Well, as I said, he didn't make very many comments. I think there were one or two times he asked me what I saw, and then he was quiet for the most part."

"Was this unusual?"

"Well, no, actually. He never commented unless I

was doing something wrong. Then he'd say, 'What do you see?' Or sometimes, to test me, he'd *let* me go through a stop sign, for example, and then tell me about it afterward."

"But this afternoon, there weren't many comments?"

"No."

"He just sat there."

"Well, yes."

"Before the woman stepped off the curb, did he ask you what you saw?"

"No."

"Did he hit the brake on his side of the car?"

"No."

Andrew Newell didn't come out of it until eight forty-five that night.

Detective Second Grade Carl Williams sat on the edge of a desk in the lieutenant's office, and watched the man trying to shake the cobwebs loose from his head. Blinking into the room. Seeing Carl, blinking again. No doubt wondering where he was and who this big black dude was sitting on the edge of the desk.

"Mr. Newell?"

"Mmm."

"Andrew Newell?"

"Mmm."

"What are you on, Mr. Newell?"

"What?"

"What'd you take, sir, knocked you on your ass that way?"

Newell blinked again.

Go ahead, say it, Carl thought.

"Where am I?" Newell asked.

Bingo.

"Raleigh Station, River Close PD," Carl said. "What kind of controlled substance did you take, man?"

"Who the hell are you?"

"Carl Williams, Detective Second, pleased to meet you. Tell me what kind of drug you took, knocked you out that way."

"I don't know what you're talking about."

Good-looking white man sitting in the lieutenant's black leather chair, blondish going gray, pale eyes bloodshot after whatever it was he'd taken. Coming out of it almost completely now, looking around the room, realizing he was in some kind of police facility, the lieutenant's various trophies on his bookshelves, the framed headlines from the *River Close Herald* when Raleigh Station broke the big drug-smuggling case three years ago. Blinking again. Still wondering what this was all about. Tell him, Carl thought.

He told him.

"According to what we've got, you were giving Rebecca Patton a driving lesson this afternoon when she ran into a woman. We don't yet know her name. She's in critical condition at Gardner General. Car was equipped with dual brakes. You were the licensed driver in the vehicle, but you didn't hit the brake on your side of the car because you were too stoned either to see the woman stepping off the curb or to react in time to avoid the accident. Now I have to tell you seriously here, Mr. Newell, that if the girl didn't know you were under the influence, if she had put her trust in you as her instructor and, in effect, you broke this trust, and this accident occurred, then most likely—and I'm not speaking for the State Attorney here—but most likely you would be the person considered culpable under the law. So it might be a good idea for you to tell me just when you took this drug, whatever it was, and why you knowingly got into a vehicle while under—"

"I didn't take any damn drug," Newell said. "I want a lawyer right this goddamn minute."

Working in the dark on Grove Avenue, playing his flashlight over the leaves on the lawn and in the gutter, Joseph Bisogno kept searching for the red handbag he'd seen the woman carrying just before the car hit her. The police had given up finding it about a half-hour ago, but Joseph knew it was important to them, otherwise they wouldn't have been turning over every leaf in the neighborhood looking for it.

Joseph was sixty-eight years old, a retired steel worker from the days when River Close was still operating the mills and polluting the atmosphere. These days the mills were gone and the town's woman mayor had campaigned on a slogan of "Clean Air, Clean Streets". She was about Joseph's age. He admired her a great deal because she was doing something with her life. Joseph had the idea that if he found the handbag, he might become a key figure in this big case the police were working. Newspaper headlines. "Retired Steelworker Key to Accident." Television interviews. "Tell us, Mr. Bisogno, did you notice the woman *before* the car struck her?" "Well, I'll tell you the truth, it all happened so fast . . ."

But, no, it hadn't happened that fast at all.

He'd been out front raking leaves when he saw the woman coming out of the church across the street, Our Lady of Sorrows, the church he himself attended every now and then when he was feeling particularly pious and holy, which was rarely. He enjoyed exercising out of doors, made him feel healthier than when he worked out on the bedroom treadmill. Mowing the lawn, picking weeds, raking leaves the way he'd been doing today, this kind of activity made him feel not like sixty-eight but forty-seven, which was anyway the age he thought of himself as being. Think of yourself as forty, then you'll feel like forty, his wife used to say. But that was before she got cancer.

He was willing to bet a thousand dollars that Mayor Rothstein thought of herself as forty-seven. Good-looking woman, too. Jewish woman. He liked Jewish women—had dated a Jewish girl named Hedda Gold when he was seventeen; she certainly knew how to kiss. Mayor Rothstein had hair as black as Tessie's hair had been before she passed away seven years ago. Maybe if he found the handbag, the mayor would ask him to head up a committee, give him something to do with his life other than mourning Tessie all the time—poor, dear Tessie.

The woman had come down the church steps, red coat flapping open in a mild autumn breeze, red handbag to match, blue skirt and white blouse under it, blue jacket, head bent as if she had serious thoughts on her mind. Leaves falling everywhere around her. Coins from heaven, Tessie used to say. He wondered if Mayor Rothstein believed in heaven; he certainly didn't. Next door, his neighbor had already started a small fire of leaves at the curb. Woman coming up the path from the church now, turning left where the path joined the sidewalk, coming toward where Joseph, on the other side of the street, was raking his leaves.

He thought . . .

For a moment, he thought the car was slowing down because the driver had seen the woman approaching the curb. A blue Ford, coming into the street slowly, cautiously. But then he realized this was a beginning driver, big yellow and black plate on the front bumper, STUDENT DRIVER, the woman stepping off the curb unheedingly, head still bent, the car speeding up as if the driver hadn't seen her after all. And then, oh God, he almost yelled to the woman, almost shouted, *Watch* it! The car, the woman, they . . . he *did* shout this time; yelled "Lady!" at the top of his lungs, but it was too late. The car hit her with a terrible wrenching thud, metal against flesh, and the woman went up into the air, legs flying, arms flying, the collision throwing her onto his neighbor's leaf fire at the curb, the shrieking of brakes, the driver leaning on her horn too late, too late, all of it too late.

The girl driving the car did not get out.

Neither did the man sitting beside her.

The girl put her head on the steering wheel, not looking at Joseph as he dragged the woman off the fire and rolled her onto the lawn. Joseph went inside to call the police. When he came out again, the girl still had her head on the wheel. The woman's red coat was charred where the flames had got to it.

He remembered all of it now.

Visualized it all over again. The woman going up into the air, legs and arms wide, as if she were trying to fly, arms going up into the air . . .

The handbag.

Yes.

Flying out of her hands, going up, up . . .

He suddenly knew where it was.

Newell's attorney didn't get to Raleigh Station until almost ten o'clock that night. His name was Martin Leipman; a smart young man Carl had met on several prior occasions, usually while testifying in court. He was wearing a shadow-striped black suit with a white shirt and a maroon tie that looked like a splash of coagulated blood. He had no objection to Carl reading Miranda to his client—as why would he?—and he listened silently while Carl ascertained that Newell had understood everything he'd explained, and was ready to proceed with answering the questions put to him. Since this had got so serious all of a sudden, Carl had also requested a police stenographer to record whatever Newell might have to say about the accident.

"You understand we can call this off anytime you say, don't you?" Leipman asked him.

"I do," Newell said.

"Just so you know. Go ahead, Detective."

Carl said, "Do you remember anything that happened on Grove and Third this afternoon?"

"No, I don't," Newell said.

"You don't remember the automobile striking that woman?"

"I don't."

"You don't remember the responding police officers asking you your name?"

"No, I don't."

"Do you remember taking any drug that would have put you in this altered state?"

"No."

"Tell me what you do remember?"

"Starting when?"

"Starting when you got into that car."

"That was after school. I teach Art Appreciation at Buckley High, and I give driving lessons after classes, twice a week. Rebecca Patton is one of my students. She had a lesson today, at ten minutes to three. I don't know who's on the schedule until I see the chart posted in the Driver's Ed office. I go there after my last class, look at the chart and then go out to the trainer car. I was waiting in the Ford at a quarter to three, behind the area where the busses pull in. She knew where to go. She began taking lessons with me over the summer vacation, started at the beginning of August actually . . ."

. . . actually, he's known Rebecca since the term before, when she and her father moved from Washington, D.C. to River Close. Art Appreciation is what is known as a crap course at Buckley High, a *snap* course if one wishes to be politically correct, but Rebecca takes it more seriously than many of the other students do, going to the public library on her own to take out books on the old masters, copying pictures from them by hand . . .

"I'm certain she would have gone to a museum if River Close had one, but of course we don't . . ."

. . . so the library had to suffice. She brings her drawings in every week—the class meets only once a week—and asks specific questions about composition and perspective, and color and design, but especially about tension, playing back to him his theory that all works of art are premised on the tension the artist generates within the prescribed confines of the canvas, the painting tugging at the frame in all directions to provide the thrill a spectator feels in the presence of genius.

"I got to know her a little better in August," Newell said, "when we began the driving lessons. She told me she wanted to do something creative with her life. She didn't know quite what, whether it'd be music, or art, or even writing, but *something*. She'd just turned sixteen, but she already knew that she didn't plan to spend her life as a bank teller or a telephone operator, she had to do something that required imagination. She told me I'd been responsible for that. My class. What I taught in my class."

"How'd you feel about that, Mr. Newell?" Carl asked.

"I was flattered. And I felt . . . well, that I'd done my job. I'd inspired a young mind to think creatively. That's important to me. When I'm teaching art, I always ask my students 'What do you see?' I want them to scrutinize any given painting and tell me in detail what they're seeing. That's how I forge a link between my students and the artist, by asking them to actually *see* what the artist saw while he was executing the work. I try to expand their horizons. I teach them to dare. I teach them to . . ."

"Let's get back to this afternoon, shall we?" Carl said.

"We've already covered this afternoon," Leipman said. "Unless you've got something new to add."

"Counselor, I still don't know what your client took."

"I told you . . ."

"He told you . . ."

"Then how'd he get in the condition he was in?"

A knock sounded discreetly on the door.

"Come in," Carl said.

Johnny Bicks, the third man on the squad's afternoon shift, poked his head around the door. "Talk to you a minute?" he asked.

"Sure," Carl said, and went out into the hall with him.

"Some guy just came in with what he claims is the victim's handbag," Johnny said.

"Where is he?"

"Downstairs, at the desk. I already told Katie."

"Thanks," Carl said. He opened the door to the lieutenant's office, leaned into the room and said, "Excuse me a moment, I'll be right back," and then closed the door and headed for the steps leading downstairs.

The man standing with Katie at the muster desk was telling her that he'd found the bag in one of the trees on Frank Pollack's lawn; his neighbor's lawn. Caught in like one of those forks in the branches, you know? Hard to see because it was red and so were the leaves all around it. Besides, the police officers had been searching the *ground*, you know? Nobody had thought to look up in the trees.

Katie asked the desk sergeant if he had any gloves back there, and he reached under the desk and handed her a pair of somewhat filthy white cotton gloves that had been used in accepting evidence two or three times before, she guessed. As she pulled on the gloves, she realized Mr. Bisogno here had already handled the bag but no sense adding insult to injury.

"How do you know it's the victim's?" Carl asked.

"I saw her carrying it," Bisogno said. "I'm the one told the officers she was carrying a red handbag."

Katie was reaching into the bag for the woman's wallet.

"You witnessed the accident?" Carl asked.

"I did."

Katie opened the wallet.

The phone on the muster desk was ringing.

"Raleigh Station, Sergeant Peters."

Katie pulled out the woman's driver's license.

"Just a second," Peters said. "Katie, for you. It's somebody at Gardner General."

She took the phone.

"Detective Logan," she said.

"This is Dr. Hagstrom in the Emergency Room at Gardner," a man's voice said.

"Yes, Dr. Hagstrom?"

"The Jane Doe we received at three fifty this afternoon?"

"Yes?"

"She's dead," Hagstrom said.

"Thank you," Katie said, and handed the phone back to Peters. "We've got a homicide," she told Carl.

Carl nodded.

Katie looked at the license in her hand.

The name on it was Mary Beth Newell.

The State Attorney who came to Raleigh Station that night at twenty to eleven was dressed in blue tailored slacks and jacket, no blouse under it, a Kelly green silk scarf at her throat picking up the virtually invisible shadow stripe of the suit. Alyce Hart was wearing blue French-heeled shoes as well, no earrings, no make-up except lipstick. Her brown hair was cut in a wedge that gave a swift look to her angular face, as if she were a schooner cutting through the wind. Katie liked everything about her but the way she chose to spell her first name. Carl liked her because he felt she thought like a man, which Alyce might have considered a dubious compliment. The three of them had worked together before; this was a small town.

"Breathalyzer was negative, right?" she asked.

"Yeah," Carl said.

"So what was he on?"

"Who knows?"

"Whatever it was, he's wide awake now," Katie said.

"Can we do a blood test?" Carl asked.

"Under Miranda, you mean?" Alyce said.

"Yeah."

"Not without his consent. Nothing I'd like better than to see what kind of juice is running through his veins, have him pee for us, too. But we'd need a court order for that, and we can't get one till he's arraigned. This was New York, Chicago, any other big bad city, we'd find an open court, have him arraigned tonight. River Close, though, just *try* to wake up some judge this hour of the night. We'll be lucky if he's arraigned by two, three tomorrow afternoon."

"Which may be too late," Katie said.

"Depending on what kind of shit he took," Carl said.

"If we can't show he was on *something*," Alyce said, "we've got no case."

"Well, we've got witnesses at the scene," Carl said.

"The girl's a witness, too," Katie said.

"Sure, but Newell's attorney might . . ."

"No question," Carl said.

"Right, claim he . . ."

"You can bet the farm on it," Alyce said. "He'll say the *accident* caused it. Shock, whatever. Couldn't walk, couldn't talk, couldn't remember his own name. Anyway, let's charge him and hold him. We may be able to get an early-morning arraignment. If not, we pray it was a drug with a long half-life. You agree with vehicular manslaughter?"

"I wish we could go for reckless," Carl said. "Guy pops pills, and then knowingly gets in a car with a *learner?* He's not only risking *her* life, he's courting disaster with everybody on the street."

"Let me offer the grand jury a choice," Alyce said. "Shoot for reckless manslaughter, settle for vehicular. How does that sound?"

"Good to me," Katie said.

"Me, too," Carl said.

"Let's get some sleep," Alyce said.

Don't let the bimbo answer, Katie thought.

She was sitting at the kitchen counter, sipping a Scotch and soda. The clock on the wall read three minutes to midnight. The phone kept ringing. Three, four, not the bimbo, she prayed.

"Hello?"

The bimbo.

"Let me talk to Stephen, please," she said.

"Who's this?"

"Mrs. Logan," she said.

"His mother?"

Sure, his mother, Katie thought.

Who happens to be dead.

"His *wife*," she said, hitting the word hard.

"Oh."

Long pause.

"Just a sec, OK?"

Sounding like a teeny bopper. Twenty-two years old, Katie thought. The minute hand on the wall clock lurched. Eleven fifty-eight. My how the time flies when you're having . . .

"Hello?"

"Stephen?"

"Yes?"

"Katie."

"Yes, Katie. Do you know what time it is?"

"I spoke to my attorney today . . ."

"Katie, we're not supposed to be doing this."

"Doing what?"

"Talking. The attorneys are supposed to do all the talking."

"Oh dear, am I breaking the law?" she asked.

"You know you're not breaking the law. But . . ."

"Then hear me out. We sent you a counter-proposal last week, and we haven't yet heard from you. I'm eager to get on with this, Stephen. I thought you were, too. Instead . . ."

"I am."

"That's what I imagined. You're the one who left, Stephen."

"Katie, I really think we should let the lawyers handle this, is what I think, really."

"I really think you should tell me what's taking you so long to study a one-page document, is what *I* think, really."

"Katie . . ." he said.

And hesitated.

She waited.

"Give me a little time, OK?" he said softly. "Please."

And all at once she was bewildered.

In bed that night, all night long, she kept remembering. Because, honestly, you know, she'd had no clue. Smart cop, first in her class at the academy, promoted to detective after a year on the force when she'd walked into a silent-alarm holdup and apprehended two guys twice her size who were wanted for armed robbery in Indiana, a hell of a long way away, but who was measuring? Smart detective. Had no clue at all that Stephen was cheating on her.

Well, married to the same guy for ten years, who would have guessed? Such a lovely couple, everyone said. High-school sweethearts, everyone said. She'd waited for him while he was in the army, waited for him when he was called up again and sent to yet another distant nation. There was always something to defend, she guessed, honor or oil or some damn thing. But, oh, how handsome he'd looked on the day they were married, Captain Stephen Gregory Logan, in his dress uniform, Miss Katharine Kyle Byrne, all in white, though certainly no virgin. Well, high-school sweethearts, you know. Met him when she was sixteen.

Who would have guessed? Not a clue.

There were the hours, of course.

A policeman's lot is not a happy one, the man once wrote and he'd been right. The graveyard shift was the worst. You wouldn't think there'd be much crime in a small city like River Close but there were drugs everywhere in America these days, and drugs moved day and night, so you had to have round the clock shifts, and you had to have cops who caught those shifts, on rotation, every three months. Whenever she jammed what was officially called "the morning shift", Katie left for work at eleven fifteen to get to the squadroom at a quarter to midnight, and didn't get home till a quarter past eight, by which time Stephen had already left for work. During those three months, she saw him maybe five, six hours a day. That wasn't too good for the marriage, she realized now, but who would have guessed then? They're so much in love, everyone said.

So last month, she gets home from a long hard afternoon shift, four to midnight, gets home at about a quarter to one in the morning, and he's sitting in his pajamas in the living room, the lights out, a drink in his hand, and he tells her he's leaving.

Leaving? she says.

She doesn't know what he means at first. Well, the

thought is inconceivable, really. His job doesn't call for travel, he's never been *sent* anywhere in all the years of their marriage, so what does he mean, he's leaving? He's a vice president at the bank. In fact it was *his* bank the two hoods from Indiana were trying to rob that day she caught the squeal, away back then when she was twenty-five and riding shotgun in a patrol car with Carl Williams. She always kidded Stephen that he got his promotion to vice president only because she thwarted the hold-up. So what does he mean, he's leaving?

You, he says. I'm leaving you.

Come on, she says, I had a hard day.

Irish sense of humor, right?

Wrong.

He was leaving her.

The police had confiscated the training vehicle the school used for its Driver's Ed course. Technicians from the lab had searched it for evidence that Newell—as instructor and supervisor—had, in effect, been "driving" the car in violation of subdivision four of section 1192 of the Vehicle and Traffic Law, which stated: "No person shall operate a motor vehicle while the person's ability to operate such a vehicle is impaired by the use of a drug as defined in this chapter." The drugs referred to were listed in the Public Health Law and constituted a virtual pharmacology of every opiate, opium derivative, hallucinogenic substance and stimulant known to man. And woman, too, Katie thought.

On Thursday morning, the day after the fatal accident, they drove over to Our Lady of Sorrows in one of the Pontiac sedans set aside for the Raleigh Station's detectives. Carl was driving, Katie was riding shotgun beside him.

"Guess what Annie cooked again last night?" Carl asked.

"Asparagus," Katie said.

"Asparagus," Carl said. "We're married six years, she *knows* I hate asparagus, but she keeps making asparagus. I told her why do you keep making asparagus when you know I hate it? First she says, "It's good for you." I tell her I don't *care* if it's good for me, I don't like the taste of it. So she says, "You'll *get* to like the taste of it." So I tell her I'm thirty-seven years old, I've been hating asparagus for thirty-seven years, I am *never* going to like the taste of it. You know what she says next?"

"What?" Katie asked.

"She says, 'Anyway, you *do* like it.' Can you believe that? I'm telling her I hate it, she tells me I like it. So I tell her one more time I *hate* asparagus, please don't make asparagus again, I *hate* it! So she says, 'When you get to be President of the United States, you won't have to eat asparagus. Meanwhile, it's good for you.' "

"That was broccoli."

"Just what I told her."

"There's the church," Katie said.

* * *

Bright morning sunlight was flooding the churchyard as they entered it through an arched wooden door leading from the church proper. Katie had expected to find Father McDowell on his knees in prayer. Saying matins, she imagined, wasn't that the one they said in the morning? The good father was, in fact, on his knees—but he was merely gathering flowers. Katie guessed he was a man in his early seventies, with a ruddy face which led her to believe he enjoyed a touch of the sacrificial wine every now and again. He greeted them warmly and told them at once that he himself had planted the mums he was now cutting for the altar. Planned the garden so that it bloomed all through the spring, summer and autumn months. The mums he was carefully placing in a wicker basket were yellow and white and purple and brown. They reminded Katie of Stephen, damn him! Excuse me, father, she thought.

"We're here to ask about a woman named Mary Beth Newell," she said. "We have reason to believe she was here at Our Lady of Sorrows yesterday. Would you remember her?"

"Yes, of course," McDowell said.

He snipped another stem, carefully placing stem and bloom alongside the others in the basket.

A football game. Stephen bringing Katie a bright orange mum to pin to her white cheerleader's sweater. The big letter B on the front of the sweater. For Buckley High.

"Is it true her husband has been arrested for killing her?" McDowell asked.

"He's been charged with vehicular homicide, yes, Father."

"But why? I understand a young girl was driving."

"That's true. But he was the licensed driver."

"It still seems . . ."

"The girl didn't know he was under the influence. State attorney believes the fault was his. *Did* Mrs. Newell come here yesterday?"

"She did."

"Can you tell us what time she got here?"

"Around two fifteen, two twenty."

"And left when?"

"An hour or so later."

They were here to learn whether or not the priest had seen the accident. They were building a list of reliable witnesses, the more the merrier. But McDowell's response stopped Katie cold. Her next question should have been, "Did you see her leaving the church?" Instead, she said, "Mrs. Newell spent a full *hour* with you?"

"Well, almost, yes."

Katie suddenly wondered why.

"Father," she said, "we know Mrs. Newell lived in St. Matthew's parish, some ten blocks from here."

"That's right."

"Is that where she worships?"

"I have no idea."

"Well, does she worship here?"

"No, she doesn't."

"Then what was she doing here, Father?"

"She'd been coming to me for spiritual guidance."

"Are you saying that today wasn't the *only* time she . . . ?"

"I can't tell you anything more, I'm sorry."

Katie knew all about privileged communication, thanks. But she was Irish. And she sniffed something in the wind.

"Father," she said, "no one's trying to pry from you whatever . . ."

McDowell was Irish, too.

"I'm sorry," he said, and snipped another stem as though he were decapitating someone possessed by the devil. Katie figured he was signaling an end to the conversation. Gee, Father, tough, she thought.

"Father," she said, "we don't want to know *what* you talked about . . ." Like hell we don't, she thought. ". . . but if you can tell us when she first came to see you."

"Is that why you're here?" McDowell said. "To invade a dead woman's privacy?" Wagging his head scornfully, he rose from where he was kneeling, almost losing his balance for a moment, but regaining it at once, his prized basket of cut flowers looped over his arm. Standing, he seemed to be at least six-feet tall. "She got here at around two fifteen," he repeated, "and left about an hour later. Does that help you?"

"Sure, but when's the *first* time she came here?" Carl asked.

He'd been silent until now, letting Katie carry the ball. But sometimes a little muscle helped. Unless you were dealing with a higher authority. Like God.

"I'm sorry, I can't tell you that," McDowell said.

So they double-ganged him.

"Did she spend an hour *each* time she visited you?" Katie asked.

"How many times *did* she visit, anyway?" Carl asked.

McDowell shook his head in disbelief. He was striding swiftly toward the entrance to the church now, the basket of flowers on his arm, the black skirts of his cassock swirling about his black trousers and highly polished black shoes. They kept pace with him, one on either side.

"She wasn't here to discuss her *husband*, was she?" Carl asked.

"Some problem her *husband* had?" Katie asked.

"Like a *drug* problem?" Carl asked.

McDowell stopped dead in his tracks. Pulling himself up to his full height, he said with dignity, "The only problems Mary Beth discussed with me were her own. Good day, detectives."

And went into his church.

So now they knew that Mary Beth Newell had problems.

Just before noon, Alyce Hart called the squadroom to say that Newell still hadn't been arraigned and if there were any further questions they wanted to ask, they'd best do it now. "The irony of our judicial system," she said, "is that we can ask the accused anything we want *before* he's arraigned, but after that we need his lawyer's permission to talk to him."

Katie wasn't quite sure what "irony" meant, exactly. Besides, she couldn't think of anything she wanted to ask except what kind of dope Newell had taken and when he'd taken it.

At a quarter past one, the phone on her desk rang again. She picked up, identified herself, and listened as a member of the search team told her that the steering wheel had yielded no evidence that Rebecca Patton had, in fact, been driving the car when it hit Mary Beth Newell. Any prints on the wheel were hopelessly overlayed and smeared because too damn many students used the same training vehicle. The techs had also found palm and fingerprints on the driver's side dashboard, presumably left there by the several instructors who used the same car and who'd reached out protectively and defensively whenever a student's reaction time was a bit off. But these, too, were smeared or superimposed one upon the other, and did nothing to prove that Andrew Newell was effectively unconscious at the time of the accident.

Katie kept listening.

The next thing he said puzzled her.

At first she thought he'd said they'd found *cocaine* in the car. She *thought* he'd said, "We also found a cup with a little *coke* in it." Which was what he *had* said, but at the same time *hadn't* said.

A moment later, she learned that what he'd *actually* said was, "We also found a cup with a little *Coke* in it." Coke with a capital C. Coca *Cola* was what he was telling her. In the Ford's center console cup holder on the passenger side, they had found a medium-sized plastic cup with the red and white Coca Cola logo on it, which cup they had immediately tested.

Katie held her breath.

"Nothing but Coca Cola in it," the tech said. "But the guy sitting there could have used it to wash down whatever shit he ingested. A possibility, Kate."

But . . .

He didn't have anything to drink while we were driving, so how could he be drunk?

How indeed? Katie wondered.

Katie got to the school at two twenty that afternoon. She went directly to the general office, showed a twenty-year-old brunette her shield and ID card, and asked for a copy of Rebecca Patton's program. The girl hesitated.

"Something wrong?" Katie asked.

"Nothing," the girl said, and went to the files.

Katie waited while she photocopied the program. It told her that Rebecca would be in an eighth-period French class till the end of the school day.

"Where's the Driver's Ed office?" she asked.

"What do you need *there*?" the girl asked.

Katie looked at her.

"Down the hall," the girl said at once, "second door on the left. You're trying to send Mr. Newell to jail, aren't you?"

"Yes," Katie said, and walked out.

What she needed in the Driver's Ed office was a feel of the place. This was where Andrew Newell came at the end of each school day to consult the chart that told him which student would be driving that day. This was where he'd come yesterday, before getting into the car that would run down his wife. Here was the wall. Here was the chart. Here were the teachers' names and the students' names. Was this the room in which he'd ingested the drug—whichever the hell drug it was—that had, minutes later, rendered him incompetent?

"You're the detective, aren't you?" a man's voice said.

Katie turned from the wall chart.

"Saw you on television last night." He was sprawled in an easy chair, open newspaper on his lap. "Right after Andy was charged," he said. "Eleven o'clock news. The red hair," he explained.

Katie nodded.

"Ed Harris," he said. "No relation."

She must have looked puzzled.

"The movie star," he said. "Ed Harris. Besides, he's bald."

This Ed Harris was not bald. He had thick black hair, graying at the temples, brown eyes behind dark-rimmed eyeglasses. He rose and extended his hand. Katie guessed he was half an inch short of six feet. Forty, forty-two, or thereabouts. Lean and lanky, like Abe Lincoln. Same rangy look. She took his hand.

"Are you going to send Andy to jail for the rest of his life?"

"Hardly," she said, and almost shook her head in

wonder. Their case was premised on the presumption that Newell had knowingly entered the training car while under the influence of a drug that had rendered him incapable of performing in his supervisory capacity. This constituted a criminally negligent act which had caused the death of another person. But the penalty for vehicular manslaughter in the second degree was only imprisonment not to exceed seven years. "If he's found guilty," she said, "the maximum . . ."

"I sincerely hope he won't be."

"Well, *if* he's convicted, the maximum sentence would be seven years. He could be out in two and a third."

"Piece of cake, right?"

Katie said nothing.

"Two and a third *days* would destroy him," Harris said.

She was thinking. If you can't do the time, don't do the crime. She still said nothing.

"For a lousy accident, right?" Harris said. "Accidents *do* happen, you know."

"Especially if a person's under the influence."

"Andy doesn't drink."

"Ever see him stoned?"

"Andy? Come on. If you knew him, you'd realize how ridiculous that sounds."

"I take it you're good friends."

"*Very* good friends."

"Do you know Rebecca, too?"

"Sure, she's in my algebra class."

"Is she a good student?"

"One of the best. Smart as hell, curious, eager to learn. And from what Andy tells me, a good driver, too."

"Not good enough. That's why there's a brake pedal on the instructor's side of the car."

"Let me tell you something," Harris said, and immediately looked up at the wall clock. She had seen his name on the chart for a driving lesson at two fifty with a student named Alberico Jiminez. The clock now read two thirty-five. In five minutes, Rebecca would be coming out of her French class. Katie didn't want to miss her.

"Andy and I both teach Driver's Ed," Harris said. "The classes are two hours long, twice a week. I teach them on Mondays and Thursdays, Andy teaches them on Wednesdays and Fridays. This is class time, you understand, not road time. Four hours a week. We try to teach *responsible* driving, Miss Logan, and we spend a great deal of time on how substance abuse affects ability and perception. These are teenagers, you know. Some of them drink, some of them smoke dope. We're all aware of that. Rebecca would have known in a minute if Andy had been under the influence. She knows all the signs, we've been over them a hundred times."

"We have witnesses who saw him staggering, saw him—"

"Your witnesses are wrong."

"My witnesses are police officers."

Harris gave her a look.

"Right," Katie said, "we're out to frame the entire nation."

"Nobody said that. But you know, Miss Logan . . ."

"Newell *should* have hit the brake. The responsibility was his."

"No. If anyone was responsible, it was Mary Beth. She's the one who wasn't looking where she was going. She's the one who stepped off that curb and into the car."

"How can you possibly know *what* she did?"

"I read the papers, I watch television. There were witnesses besides your police officers."

"And she was your friend . . ."

"She was."

"Any idea what might have been troubling her?"

"Who says she was troubled?"

"You didn't detect anything wrong?"

"No. Wrong? No."

A bell sounded, piercing, insistent, reminding her that this was, in fact, a school, and that she was here to see a student.

As she turned to leave, Harris said, "You're making a mistake here, Miss Logan. If nobody hit that brake, there simply wasn't *time* to hit it."

"Good talking to you, Mr. Harris," Katie said.

"Ed," he said. "Don't hurt him."

Rebecca came down the front steps of the school at a quarter to three, her books hugged to the front of her pale-blue sweater. Girls and boys were streaming down the steps everywhere around her, flowing toward where the idling yellow school busses were parked. A bright buzz of conversation, a warm consonance of laughter floated on the crisp October air.

"Hey, hi," she said, surprised.

"Hi, Rebecca. Give you a ride home?"

"Well . . . sure," she said.

Katie fell into step beside her. Together, they walked in silence across the curving drive and into the parking lot. Leaves were falling everywhere around them, blowing on the wind, rustling underfoot. Katie reached into her tote bag. Her keys were resting beside the walnut stock of a .38 caliber Detectives Special. She dug them out and unlocked the door of the car on the passenger side.

"I sometimes think I'll never get in another car again," Rebecca said.

"It wasn't your fault," Katie said.

"It wasn't his, either."

"Tell me something. When you said . . ."

"I don't want to say anything that will hurt Mr. Newell."

"His negligence killed someone," Katie said flatly.

"You don't know he was drugged. Maybe he had a stroke or something. Or a heart attack. Something. It didn't have to be drugs. You just don't know for sure."

"That's what we're trying to find out."

"He must be *heart*broken, his own *wife*!"

"It doesn't matter who it was, he—"

"*I* was the one driving! Why should Mr. Newell . . . ?"

"You were in his custody."

"I was *driving*!"

"And he was *stoned*!" Katie said sharply. "His responsibility was to—"

"Please, please, don't."

"Rebecca, listen to me!"

"What?"

Her voice catching. She's going to start crying again, Katie thought.

"Did you know he was drugged?" she asked.

"No."

"Then you're not culpable, can you understand that? And protecting him would be a horrible mistake. I want you to answer one question."

"I can't, please, I—"

"You *can*, damn it!"

Her voice crushed the autumn stillness. Leaves fell like colored shards of broken glass. In the distance there was the rumble of the big yellow busses pulling away from the school.

"You told me Andrew Newell didn't drink anything while you were driving," Katie said. "Is that still your recollection?"

Silence.

"Rebecca?"

The girl hugged her schoolbooks to her chest, head bent, blonde hair cascading on either side of her face. The sounds of the busses faded. Leaves fell, twisted, floated. They stood silently, side by side, in a stained-glass cathedral of shattered leaves. Gray woodsmoke drifted on the air from somewhere, everywhere. Katie suddenly remembered all the autumns there ever were.

"We stopped for a Coke," Rebecca said.

"This was right after the lesson began," Katie told Carl. They were sitting side by side at wooden desks in the squadroom. Most of the furniture here went back to the early forties when River Close first established a detective division. Until that time, any big case here, the chief had to call in detectives from the county seat up Twin River Junction. "Say five after three; Rebecca didn't check her watch. Newell said he was thirsty, and directed her to the drive-in on Olive and High. They ordered a Coke for him at the drive-in window, and were on their way in five seconds flat. Newell kept sipping the Coke as they drove."

"Did Rebecca see him popping any pills?"

"No."

"So all we've got is the tech's guess."

"Plus Newell stoned at the scene some fifteen minutes later."

Both of them fell silent.

At four this afternoon, Newell had finally been arraigned, and they'd got their court order for blood and urine tests. They were waiting for the results now. Meanwhile, they had statements from all the various witnesses, but that was all they had.

It was now a quarter past five and dusk was coming on fast.

At six thirty, just as Katie and Carl were packing it in, the phone on her desk rang. It was Alyce Hart, calling to say that Newell's blood had tested positive for secobarbital sodium.

"Brand name's Seconal," she said. "Not often prescribed as a sedative these days. From what the lab tells me, fifty milligrams is the sedative dose. For Newell to have presented the effects he did at the scene, he had to've ingested at least three times that amount."

"A hundred and fifty mills."

"Right. That's the hypnotic dose for a man of his weight. Full hypnotic effect of the drug usually occurs fifteen to thirty minutes following oral or rectal administration."

"Think somebody shoved it up his ass?"

"Unlikely. Effects would've been very similar to alcoholic inebriation. Imperfect articulation of speech, failure of muscular coordination, clouded sensorium."

"What's that?"

"Sensorium? State of consciousness or mental awareness. I had to ask, too."

Which was another thing Katie liked about Alyce.

"How long would these effects last?" she asked.

"Three to eight hours."

"Fits Newell, doesn't it?"

"Oh, doesn't it just?"

"Think he was an habitual user?"

"Who cares? We've got a case now, Katie."

"We've also got what he washed the pills down with."

"Oh?"

Katie told her about Newell stopping to buy a Coke just before the accident. She also mentioned that she'd been to Our Lady of Sorrows and had learned that Mary Beth Newell had taken her problems to the priest there, seeking spiritual guidance.

"Problems. What kind of problems?"

"He wouldn't say. But Our Lady of Sorrows isn't her parish."

"What is her parish?"

"St. Matthew's."

"How far away?"

"Ten blocks."

"Mm," Alyce said, and was silent for a moment. "What are you thinking, Katie?"

"Well . . . if Newell *knew* his wife was troubled about something, his lawyers might claim her state of mind was such that she caused the accident herself."

"Yeah, go ahead."

"By not paying attention to where she was going. Or even by deliberately stepping into the car's path."

"It's a defense, yes," Alyce said thoughtfully.

"So, what I was thinking is maybe we should try to find out exactly *what* was bothering her. Before the defense does. In fact, I thought I might drop in on her sister tomorrow morning."

"OK, but don't expect too much. This may turn out

to be nothing. Everybody has problems, Katie. Don't you have problems?"

"Me?" Katie said. "Not a worry in the world."

Thing she used to do when she and Stephen were still a proper man and wife, would be to ask him questions. "Stephen, what does 'irony' mean, exactly?" And, of course, he would tell her. He'd been telling her things ever since she was sixteen. Anything she wanted to know, she'd ask Stephen and he would tell her. So what she wanted to do *now* was pick up the phone and call him. Say, "Hi, Stephen, I hope I'm not interrupting you and your bimbo at . . . what time is it, anyway? My oh my, is it *really* one fifteen in the morning? I certainly hope I'm not intruding. But someone used the word 'irony' in my presence, and it occurred to me that although I often use that word myself, or even its sister word 'ironic' I've never been really quite sure what *either* of those words mean exactly. So, Stephen, if it's not too much trouble, I wonder . . ."

But no.

Because you see, she and Stephen were no longer proper man and wife, she and Stephen were separated, that was the irony of it, that was what was so very damn ironic about the situation. So she got out of bed in her pajamas and padded barefoot to the little room Stephen had used as a study when he still lived here, and went to the bookshelves behind what used to be his desk and found the dictionary and thumbed through it till first she found "iron" and then "ironclad" and "iron hand" and finally, bingo, there it was, "ironic". And guess what the definition was? The definition, according to Mr. Webster himself, was: "meaning the contrary of what is expressed."

Huh? she thought.

How does that . . . ?

She ran her finger down the page and found the word "irony", and its first definition seemed to echo what she'd just learned about "ironic". In which case, she wondered, what's so damn *ironic* about them not being able to question Newell after he was arraigned? But hold it, kiddies, not so fast, here came the *second* definition. Katie took a sip of Scotch. "Irony," she read out loud. "A result that is the opposite of what might be expected or considered appropriate."

So if you can question a man because you *hope* to charge him with a crime, but then you can no longer question him after he's been *charged* with that crime, she guessed that was sure enough ironic.

Yep, that's irony, she thought.

How about that, Stephen?

How about that, hon?

A fine Friday-morning mist burnt away as Katie drove through the small village of River Bend, and then into the countryside again, where narrow streams wound through glades covered with fallen leaves. She drove onto a covered bridge, the interior of her car going dark, brilliant sunlight splashing her windshield a moment later. She hoped she wouldn't get a migraine, sudden changes of light often brought them on. Stephen would fetch her two aspirin tablets and advise her to lie down at once. No migraine, please, she thought. Not now. No Stephen to offer solace, you see.

The towns, hamlets, villages and occasional city in this part of the state suffered from a watery sameness of nomenclature due to a natural abundance of rivers and lakes. Mary Beth Newell's sister was a kindergarten teacher in Scotts Falls, named after the rapids that cascaded from the southernmost end of Lake Paskonomee, some twenty miles north-east of River Close, and within shouting distance of Twin River Junction, the county seat. If Andrew Newell had been charged with reckless endangerment, his attorney most likely would have asked for a change of venue and Alyce would have had to prosecute in Twin River J, as the town was familiarly known to the locals. Even with the lesser charge, Leipman might ask that the case be moved out of River Close. Either way, Alyce would go for the jugular.

Katie found Helen Pierce in a fenced-in area behind the elementary school. Katie had spoken to her only once before, on the telephone the night they learned Mary Beth Newell was dead. She had seen only police photographs of the dead woman's body, and could not form any true opinion as to whether or not the sisters resembled each other. The woman now leading a chanting band of feathered and painted five-year-olds in what appeared to be a war dance was in her late thirties, Katie guessed, with soft brown hair and deep-brown eyes. She wore no make-up, not even lipstick. She had on a plain blue smock and Reeboks with no socks. She was also wearing a huge feathered headdress. Calling a break, she told Katie that this was an authentic Lakota Sioux ritual rain dance, and that she and the children were trying to break the twenty-seven day drought that had gripped the region.

"Keeps the foliage on the trees," she said, "but the reservoirs are down some fifty percent." She waved her feathered dancers toward a long wooden table upon which pint cartons of milk and platters of cookies had been set out. Keeping a constant eye on the children, she walked Katie to a nearby bench, where they sat side by side in dappled shade.

"Did your sister ever mention her visits to a priest at Our Lady of Sorrows?" Katie asked.

"No," Helen said at once, and turned toward her, surprised. "Why would she go there? Her church is St. Matthew's."

"The priest indicated that something was troubling her. Would she have mentioned that to you?"

"No. But why is it important?"

Katie explained what a possible defense tactic might be. Helen listened intently, shaking her head, occasionally sighing. At last, she said, "That's absurd, nothing was troubling my sister that deeply. Nothing she confided to me, anyway. Well . . . but no."

"What?"

"She and Andy were trying to have a baby. Without any luck."

"Would that have bothered her enough to . . . ?"

"Well, Andy's *attitude* might have annoyed her. But I don't think she'd have gone to a priest about it."

"What attitude?"

"He didn't want a 'damn baby', as he put it. Went along with her efforts only because she threatened to leave him if he didn't. But they argued day and night about it, even when other people were with them. He kept saying if they had a damn baby, they'd never be able to go back to Europe the way he wanted to. He studied art in Europe, you know, and his big dream was to go back there. That's what he'd been saving for, and having a baby would ruin all that. I sometimes felt the reason she couldn't conceive was because of Andy's negative stance. I know that's dumb, but it's what I thought."

"But she never once mentioned seeing Father McDowell?"

"No."

"Never mentioned whatever was troubling her?"

"Never." She was silent for a moment, and then suddenly, as if the idea had just occurred to her, she asked, "Have you looked for a diary?"

"No, did she keep . . . ?"

"Why don't you look for a diary or something?" Helen said. "She always kept a diary when we were kids. Little lock on it, kept it in her top dresser drawer, under her socks. I'll bet anything she *still* keeps one, you really should take a look." And then, all at once, she realized that she was speaking of her sister in the present tense, as if she were still alive. Her eyes clouded. "Well, we were kids," she said, and fell silent. Across the yard, the children were beginning to get restless. "This whole damn thing," she said, shaking her head, "the damn *stupidity* of it . . . the . . . the very *idea* that some smart lawyer might try to get Andy off on a ridiculous claim of . . . of . . . Mary Beth being *troubled*!"

She rose abruptly.

"Send him away," she said. "Send the son of a bitch away for life." Katie was about to explain yet another time that all you could get for vehicular homicide was a maximum of seven years. But Helen had already turned away, and in an overly loud voice she shouted, "OK, let's make *rain*!"

The request Katie typed into her computer read:

1. I am a detective of the River Close Police Department, assigned to the Raleigh Station, where I am currently investigating the vehicular homicide of Mary Beth Newell.
2. I have information based upon facts supplied to me by Father Brian McDowell, pastor of the Church of Our Lady of Sorrows in River Close, that Mrs. Newell had been coming to him "for spiritual guidance" regarding personal problems.
3. I have information based upon facts supplied to me by Mrs. Helen Pierce, the deceased's sister, that she

> kept a locked personal diary in the top drawer of her . . .

Well, now, she thought, leave us pause a moment, shall we? Am I telling the absolute truth here? On an affidavit that will be sworn to before a magistrate? True, Helen Pierce told me her sister *used* to keep a locked diary when she was a kid, *used* to keep it in the top drawer of her dresser, is what Helen told me, Your Honor, I swear to that on a stack of bibles.

But she also said, and I quote this verbatim, "I'll bet anything she *still* keeps one, you really should take a look," is what she told me. Those were her exact words. So, whereas I *do* fervently wish to send Andrew Newell away for a very long time, the son of a bitch, I don't think I'm lying or even stretching the truth here when I say that I have information—based on facts supplied by her sister, Your Honor—that Mary Beth Newell kept a locked personal diary in the top drawer of her dresser, although not under her socks.

So, Your Honor . . .

> Based upon the foregoing reliable information and upon my own personal knowledge, there is probable cause to believe that Mrs. Newell may have confided to her diary information regarding her state of mind at the time of the incident, which information would help determine whether Mrs. Newell was sufficiently troubled or distracted to

> have recklessly contributed in some measure to her own demise.

Which is exactly what Newell's lawyers would love to prove, and that's why I want to get my hands on that diary, if it exists, before they do, Your Honor.

> Wherefore, I respectfully request that the court issue a search warrant in the form annexed hereto, authorizing a search of the premises at 1220 Hanover Road, Apartment 4C, for a diary belonging to the deceased.

They tossed the apartment high and low and could not find a locked diary in Mary Beth's top dresser drawer or anyplace else. They did, however, find an appointment calendar.

In plain view, as they would later tell Alyce Hart.

Which meant they were within their rights to seize the calendar as evidence without violating the court order.

The calendar revealed that starting on the twenty-first day of August, Mary Beth Newell had scheduled appointments at two fifteen every Wednesday and Saturday afternoon, with someone she'd listed only as "McD". These meetings continued through to the day of the accident.

"Well, even beyond that," Katie said. "Take a look. She had another one scheduled for tomorrow, and another two next week. Now unless she was going to McDonald's for hamburgers, I think we can safely assume the "McD" stands for McDowell. In which case . . ."

"Let's revisit the man," Carl said.

Father McDowell was alone in a small chapel off the side portal, deep in silent prayer when they entered the church through the center doors at three that afternoon. A blazing afternoon sun illuminated the high arched stained-glass windows, washing the aisles with color. They spotted the priest at once, and waited respectfully until he made the sign of the cross and got to his feet. He stood staring at the crucifix over the altar for a moment, as though not quite finished with his Lord and Savior, adding a postscript to his prayers, so to speak, and then made the sign of the cross again, and started backing away into the main church. He turned, saw them at once, scowled with the memory of their earlier visit, and seemed ready to make a dash for the safety of the church proper—but they were upon him too swiftly; he was trapped in the tiny chapel.

"Few questions, Father," Katie said at once.

"I have business to attend to," he said.

"So do we," Carl said.

"We have Mary Beth Newell's appointment calendar," Katie said. "It shows she'd been coming to see you twice a week since the third week in August."

Father McDowell said nothing.

"That sounds pretty serious to us," Carl said. "A woman walking all the way over here, twice a week."

"What was troubling her, Father?"

"We need to know."

"Why?" he asked.

"Did Andrew Newell know she was coming here?"

From the organ loft, quite abruptly, there came the sound of thick sonorous notes, flooding the church. The glorious music, the sunlight streaming through the stained glass, the scent of incense burning somewhere, the flickering of votive candles in small red containers on the altar behind McDowell, all blended to lend the small church the sudden air of a medieval cathedral, where knights in armor came to say their last confessions before riding off to battle.

"Why was she coming to see you?" Katie asked.

"Why not her own parish?" Carl asked.

"Help us, Father," Katie said.

"Why?" he asked again.

"Because if her husband knew she was coming here, if he *knew* his wife was troubled about something . . ."

"Then his attorney might try to show she was distracted at the time of the accident . . ."

". . . walked into that car because her mind was on something else."

"Worse yet, walked into it *deliberately*."

"She was not suicidal, if that's what you're suggesting," McDowell said.

"Then tell us *what* she was."

"Help us," Katie said again.

The priest sighed heavily.

"Please," she said.

He nodded, almost to himself, nodded again and then walked into the church proper, up the center aisle to a pew some six rows back from the main altar. The detectives sat one on either side of him. As he spoke, McDowell kept his eyes on the crucifix hanging above the altar, as if begging forgiveness for breaking faith with someone who had come to him in confidence. From the organ loft, the music swelled magnificently. McDowell spoke in a whisper that cut through the laden air like a whetted knife.

"She came to see me because she suspected her husband was having an affair," he said. "She was too embarrassed to go to her parish priest."

But twice a week? Katie thought. For eight weeks? Ever since the twenty-first of August?

As McDowell tells it, at first she is uncertain, blaming herself for being a suspicious wife, wondering if her doubts have more to do with her inability to become pregnant than with what she perceives as her husband's wandering. He doesn't want a baby, she knows that; he has made that abundantly clear to her. As the weeks go by and she becomes more and more convinced that he is cheating on her, she wonders aloud and tearfully if perhaps her incessant campaign, her relentless attempts to conceive, her strict insistence on observing the demands of the calendar and the thermometer chart, haven't transmogrified what should have been a pleasurable act into an onerous experience, something dutiful and distasteful, something rigid and structured that has forced him to seek satisfaction elsewhere.

"By the end of the summer, she was positive there was another woman," McDowell said.

"Did she say who?"

"No. But she was becoming very frightened."

"Why?"

"Because someone was following her."

"She saw someone following her?"

"No, she didn't actually *see* anyone. But she felt a presence behind her. Watching her every move."

"A presence?" Carl asked, raising his eyebrows skeptically.

"Yes," McDowell said. "Someone behind her. Following her."

"Good!" Alyce said on the telephone that evening. "This only makes him more despicable!"

"You think he was the one following her?" Katie asked.

"Either him or his bimbo, who cares? Here's a woman trying to get pregnant and her darling husband's fooling around. Just *let* the defense try to show her as a troubled woman—I dare them. The trouble was her *husband*. Gets into a car stoned out of his mind and causes the death of an innocent wife who's faithfully attempting to create a family while he's running around with another woman. Seven years? The jury will want to *hang* him!"

Katie hoped she was right.

"Let's nail it down," Alyce said. "I want a minute by minute timetable, Katie. I want to know who saw the training car leaving the school parking lot at exactly what time. Who served Andrew Newell that Coke at exactly what time. Who saw Mary Beth

Newell step out of that church and start walking toward her rendezvous with death at exactly what time . . ."

Sounding like she was already presenting her closing argument to the jury . . .

". . . who saw the car approaching the crossing of Third and Grove at exactly what time. Who saw the car striking that poor woman at exactly what time. It takes fifteen to thirty minutes for Seconal to start working. OK, let's prove to a jury that he had to've swallowed the drug on the way to Grove and Third and was incapable of preventing his own wife's death! Lets prove the cheating bastard *killed* her!"

Amen, Katie thought.

The accident had taken place on Wednesday at approximately three twenty in the afternoon. This was now eleven a.m. on Saturday morning, the nineteenth day of October, and the drive-in at this hour was virtually deserted, the breakfast crowd having already departed, the lunch crowd not yet here.

Katie and Carl asked to see the manager and were told by a sixteen-year-old kid wearing a red and yellow uniform that the manager was conducting a training session just now and wouldn't be free for ten, fifteen minutes. Carl told her to inform the manager that the police were here. They ordered coffee and donuts at the counter, and carried them to one of the booths. The manager came out some three minutes later.

She was nineteen or twenty, Katie guessed, a pert

little black woman with a black plastic name tag that told them she was JENNIE DEWES, MGR. She slid in the booth alongside Carl, looked across at Katie, and said, "What's the trouble?"

"No trouble," Katie said. "We're trying to pinpoint the exact time a Coca Cola would have been purchased here on Wednesday afternoon."

Jennie Dewes, Mgr. looked at her.

"You're kidding, right?" she said.

"No, we're serious, miss," Carl said.

"You know how many Cokes we serve here every day?"

"This would've been a Coke you served sometime around three o'clock this past Wednesday," Katie said.

"You mind if I see your badges, please?" Jennie said.

Katie opened her handbag, fished out her shield in its leather fob. Carl had already flipped open his wallet.

"Okay," Jennie said, and nodded. "This would've been drive-in or counter?"

"Drive-in," Katie said.

"Three o'clock would've been Henry on the window. Let me get him."

She left the booth, and returned some five minutes later with a lanky young blond boy who looked frightened.

"Sit down, son," Carl said.

The boy sat. Sixteen, seventeen years old, Katie

guessed, narrow acne-ridden face, blue eyes wide in fear. Jennie sat, too. Four of them in the booth now. Jennie sitting beside Carl, Henry on Katie's left.

"We're talking about three days ago," Carl said. "Blue Ford Escort with a student driver plate on it, would you remember?"

"No, sir, I'm sorry, I sure don't," Henry said.

"Don't be scared, Henry," Katie said. "You're not in any trouble here."

"I'm not scared, ma'am," he said.

"Blue Ford Escort. Yellow and black student driver plates on the front and rear bumper."

"Young blonde girl would've been driving."

"Pulled in around three, ordered a Coke."

"Not at the window," Jennie said suddenly.

They all looked at her.

"If this is the right girl, I saw her inside here. Pretty white girl, blonde, sixteen, seventeen years old."

"Sixteen, yes. Brown eyes."

"Didn't notice her eyes."

"Man with her would've been older."

"Thirty-two."

"Wasn't any man with her when I saw her."

"What time was this?" Katie asked.

"Around three, like you say. She was coming out of the ladies' room. Went to the counter to pick up her order."

"Picked up a Coke at the counter?"

"*Two* of them was what she picked up. Two medium Cokes."

* * *

They found her at a little past noon in the River Close Public Library, poring over a massive volume of full-color Picasso prints. The table at which she sat was huge and oaken, with green-shaded lamps casting pools of light all along its length. There was a hush to the room. Head bent, blonde hair cascading over the open book, Rebecca did not sense their approach until they were almost upon her. She reacted with a startled gasp, and then recovered immediately.

"Hey, hi," she said.

"Hello, Rebecca," Katie said.

Carl merely nodded.

The two detectives sat opposite her at the table. A circle of light bathed the riotous Picasso print, touched Rebecca's pale hands on the open book, and Carl's darker hands flat on the table top.

"Rebecca," Katie said, "what happened to the second Coke container?"

"What?" Rebecca said, and blinked.

"You bought two Cokes," Carl said. "The techs found only one empty container in the car. What happened to the other one?"

"I guess I threw it out," Rebecca said.

"Then there *were* two containers, right?"

"I guess so. Yes, there probably were."

"Why'd you throw it out?" Katie asked.

"Well . . . because I'd finished with it."

"Rebecca . . . the container you threw out wasn't yours, was it?"

"Yes, it was. I'm sorry, I don't know what you're . . ."

"It was Mr. Newell's, wasn't it?"

"No, I distinctly remember . . ."

"The one *he* was drinking from, isn't that true?"

"No, that was in the holder. The cup holder. On the center console. I'm sorry, but I'm not following you. If you can tell me what you're looking for, maybe I can help you. But if you . . ."

"Where'd you toss the container?" Carl asked.

"Somewhere on the . . . the street, I guess. I really don't remember."

"Where on the street?"

"I don't remember the exact location. I just opened the window and threw it out."

"Was it somewhere between the drive-in and the spot where you ran down Mrs. Newell?"

"I suppose so."

"We'll look for it," Carl said.

"We'll find it," Katie said.

"So find it," Rebecca said. "What's so important about a stupid *Coke* container, anyway?"

"The residue," Katie said.

And suddenly Rebecca was weeping.

The way she tells it . . .

This was after she'd been informed of her rights, and after her attorney and her father had both warned her, begged her not to answer any questions.

But she tells it, anyway.

She is sixteen, and so she must tell it.

The video camera whirs silently as the little blonde girl with the wet brown eyes tells the camera and her lawyer and her father and the state attorney and all the assembled police officers exactly how this thing came to pass.

She supposes she fell in love with Mr. Newell . . .

She keeps referring to him as "Mr. Newell". She does not call him Andrew or Andy, which is odd when one considers the intimate nature of their relationship. But he remains "Mr. Newell" throughout her recitation. Mr. Newell and his passionate love of art, which he transmits to his students in a very personal way, "What do you see? What do you see *now*?"

And, oh, what she sees is this charming, educated man, much older than she is, true, but seeming so very *young*, burning with enthusiasm and knowledge, this sophisticated world traveler who studied in Italy and in France and who is now trapped in a shoddy little town like River Close with a wife who can only think of making babies!

She doesn't learn this, doesn't hear about his wife's . . . well, obsession, you might call it . . . until she begins taking driving lessons with him at the beginning of August. They are alone together for almost two hours each time, twice a week, and she feels confident enough to tell him all about her dreams and her desires, feels privileged when he confides to her his plans of returning to Europe one day, to Italy especially, where the light is golden and soft.

"Like you, Rebecca," he says to her one day, and puts his hand on her knee and dares to kiss her, dares to slide his hand up under her short skirt.

There are places in River Close . . .

There are rivers and lakes and hidden glades where streams are drying in the hot summer sun, no rain, the trees thick with leaves. The little blue Ford Escort hidden from prying eyes while Mr. Newell gives her lessons of quite another sort. Rebecca open and spread beneath him on the back seat. Mr. Newell whispering words of encouragement and endearment while he takes her repeatedly, twice a week. Rebecca delirious with excitement and wildly in love.

When she suggests one day toward the middle of September . . .

They are in a parched hidden glade; if only it would rain, the town needs rain so badly. Her panties are off, she is on the back seat; they have already made love, and she feels flushed and confident. He is telling her he adores her, worships her, kissing her again, calling her his blonde princess, his little blonde princess. I love you, I love you, kissing her everywhere, everywhere . . .

"Then leave your wife and marry me," she suggests. "Take me with you to Italy."

"No, no," he says, "I can't do that."

"Why not?" she says. "You love me, don't you?"

"I adore you," he says.

"Then marry me."

"I can't," he says.

"Why not?" she asks again.

"I'm already married," he says.

There is a smile on his face as he makes his little joke—I'm already married—which is supposed to explain it all to the little sophomore who was stupid enough to fall in love with the worldly art professor. How could she have been so goddamn *dumb*?

What do you see, Rebecca?

What do you see *now*?

She sees killing her.

Mr. Andrew Newell's beloved wife Mary Beth.

"At first, I could only follow her on Saturdays. I go to school, you know. But I had to figure out a way to kill her with the *car*, so he'd be blamed. I take Driver's Ed courses so I knew that the licensed driver is the one responsible in any accident. So I wanted him to be in the car with me, so he'd be blamed. That way he'd be charged with murder and get sent to prison for life.

"But I needed to know where she'd be on the days I had my driving lessons, Wednesdays and Fridays. So one week, I stayed home from school and followed her on Wednesday. She went to the church again, same as on Saturday. And the next week I stayed home on Friday and followed her, but she was just doing errands and such, it would've been too difficult to plan a way our paths would intersect. Her path and the car's path, I mean. During a driving lesson. A Wednesday driving lesson. It had to be on a Wednesday, because that's when she went to the church, you see.

"I take Driver's Ed courses, I know all about drunk driving, I figured the only way Mr. Newell could be blamed was if I got him drunk. But he didn't drink. I once brought a bottle of wine to the woods with us, this was the second time we made love. I wanted to show him how sophisticated I was, so I bought this bottle of very expensive Chardonnay, it cost me twenty-two dollars. But he wouldn't drink any, he told me he didn't drink. That was when I still thought he loved me. That was before I realized he was making a fool of me.

"There are lots of medical books in my father's library—he's a doctor, you know—books on pharmacology and toxicology, everything I needed. I started browsing the books, trying to find something I could give Mr. Newell that would make it *look* as if he was drunk when I ran her over. Make it look like *he* was the responsible party. Any of the barbiturates looked good to me. I searched through my father's bag one night and found some Seconal capsules and decided to go with them. I dropped two big red caps in his Coke before I carried it out to the car. Two hundred milligrams. I figured that would do it. The rest was easy."

"Did you intend killing her?" Alyce asked.

"Oh yes."

"Why?"

"Because he was making a fool of me. He loved her, you see, otherwise he'd have left her to marry me. I did it to pay him back. If this worked the way I wanted it to, he'd have gone to prison for life."

"Do you know what the penalty for vehicular homicide is?" Katie asked.

"Yes," she said at once. "Prison for life. Homicide is murder."

"Seven years, Rebecca."

Rebecca looked at her.

"It's seven years."

The room went utterly still.

"I didn't know that," Rebecca said.

"Well, now you do," Alyce said.

It began raining along about then.

Driving home through the rain, Katie thought how goddamn sad it was that a girl as bright and as beautiful as Rebecca could have made the tragic mistake of believing in love and romance in a time when vows no longer meant anything.

Sixteen years old, she thought. Only sixteen.

I'm in love with someone else, Katie.

I'm leaving you.

The irony, she thought, and brushed hot sudden tears from her eyes.

"Enough," she said aloud.

And drove fiercely into the storm ahead.

PETALS

Frankfurt, Germany: March 31, 1974

In the street below his window, he could hear someone singing noisily, the voice grating against the sound of the bells that came pealing across the *Hauptwache*. The singer was somewhat drunk. He slurred each lyric, laughed when he missed a word or a step, the song rising cacophonously against the distant clangor of the bells. The song trailed, ended—perhaps a corner had been turned, a building entered. There was only the faraway tolling now, and even that ceased, and the evening was still.

It was seven o'clock.

The room in which he sat watching the street was tiny, its walls covered with a bold, flower-patterned paper, peeling and yellowed except for a brown patch above the stove where grease stains had almost entirely obscured the original design. The room was cold. He had spoken to Frau Kimmel about the heat the night before, but she had merely shrugged and replied, "What can one expect for ninety marks a week, Herr Buchmann?" He repeated her shrug now in the silence of the room. What indeed could one expect for ninety marks a week? He rose to turn on the single lamp over the dresser, decided against it, and sank again into the chair near the window. On the stove, a green enamel tea kettle simmered over a low flickering flame, the room's only illumination.

Beyond his window, the evening sky was succumbing to night. Darkness hung directly above St. Catherine's, as though its spire had punctured an enormous black balloon to release a rush of blue-violet gasses that spread across the horizon behind St. Paul's and the Dom. He watched the changing sky. The sun was gone, but a faint trace of red brazened the blue behind the *Henningerturm*, and then was vanquished. A narrow band of twilight limned the horizon for an instant only and suddenly winked into blackness.

He turned sharply toward the door.

Listening intently, he leaned forward in his chair. He could hear only his own breathing now, and the steady whisper of the simmering kettle on the stove. Beyond the room, the city was silent. Outside in the corridor, there was a greater silence—contained, waiting, listening.

He watched the doorknob.

It turned.

Slowly, experimentally, it turned. He heard rather than saw the slight inward pressure of the creaking door as it strained against the jamb. Then the knob turned back to its original position again, slowly, guided by a hand rather than suddenly released. He held his breath.

There were two locks on the door, a deadbolt and a steel slip bolt not six inches above it. He watched in astonishment as first the deadbolt imploded from the door, its brass parts flying soundlessly into the room. The slip bolt burst inward next, again without a sound, seeming to leap from the door of its own volition, clanging noisily only when it struck the floor.

The door opened.

A blonde woman stood in the door frame, holding a Luger in her right hand. A silencer was attached to the muzzle of the pistol. She was wearing a black raincoat. The light from the hallway was behind her, her face in shadows. When she closed the door, there was only the low flame of the stove flickering on the blued steel of the weapon in her hand.

"*Guten Abend, Herr Stolz*," she said, and smiled.

He knew immediate fear. He did not think he would be this frightened. "I am Frederick Buchmann," he answered in German. "What do you want?"

"*Nein*," the woman replied.

"What do you want here?" he said. "What right do you have . . . ?"

"You are not Frederick Buchmann," she said in German. "You are Hans Stolz."

"I am Frederick Buchmann."

"Hans Stolz," she repeated.

"There must be some mistake."

"There is no mistake," she said. She was leaning

casually against the door now, her pose not at all threatening, the Luger pointing without apparent menace, almost as though she had forgotten it was in her hand. "I have been watching you for twelve days now, *Herr* Stolz. I know who you are, and there is no mistake."

"I am Frederick Buchmann," he insisted. "I . . ."

There was only a faint whisper of sound, not even time for him to be surprised; the bullet was unerringly accurate, he was dead before he struck the floor. The woman walked to him nonetheless, and stood over him, and fired two more silent shots into his forehead.

Then she went to the stove, turned off the gas under the tea kettle, and left the room.

Cologne, Germany: April 16, 1974

Behind him, Michael Henderson could hear streetcars rattling past in the April sunshine. He had been told Edstrand would be coming on a Number 16 car. The voice on the telephone had said, in German, "*Nummer sechzehn, verstehen sie*?" and he had replied, in English, "I understand. Number sixteen."

Michael looked at his watch.

They had told him Edstrand would be here promptly at four, but it was now a quarter past, and he was beginning to suspect something had gone wrong. Another trolley was approaching. He turned casually toward it, peering over the top edge of the daily *Koelner Stadt-Anzeiger*. The number on the front of the car was 22. He folded the newspaper and put it on the bench beside him, the banner and the headline showing. He looked at his watch again. He would wait another five minutes, that was all.

A tall blond woman appeared suddenly around the bend of the path. She was an American, Michael knew that at once—the camera bouncing jauntily on a shoulder strap, the careful but reckless hair styling, the clothes, and particularly the walk. French women insinuated their way down boulevard or avenue, Italian women crossed piazzas like pigeons in low flight, German women marched erect in four/four time to secret three/four waltzes, but American women . . . *sailed*. American women were sloops, gliding silently on frothy oceans, daring the wind to die. There was very little wind this bright April day, but the woman's blond hair floated about her shoulders with each seaborne step, as though tossed by inner breezes. There was a smile on her face. She was plainly enjoying the beauty of the day and the gardens, enjoying too her own swift sound on a self-created sea.

She stopped at a bank of yellow tulips some twenty feet from where Michael sat on the bench. She seemed one with the massed flowers, green skirt and paler green blouse, blond hair echoing stem, leaf, and petal. She swung her camera into position, threw back the leather cover, focused, adjusted, and snapped. Stepping back to appraise another angle, she went through the same ritual again, and then kneeled for a closer shot of open petals. He saw a delicate flash of lace as her skirt pulled back for just an instant, watched as her hand automatically and unconsciously tugged the skirt over her knee and then moved to the lens of the camera again. Another trolley was approaching, he turned to look at it. Number 16. He watched as passengers disembarked—an old woman wearing a pale blue suit, white gloves, and a flowered bonnet; a young matron helping her small son off the step and onto the cobbled street; and a man wearing a brown suit. The man had a newspaper folded under his arm.

"Excuse me."

He knew it was she at once, knew that *this* voice could only belong to the blond woman with the camera. He turned to look up into her face.

"Do you speak English?" she asked.

"Yes," Michael answered.

She was perhaps twenty-nine or thirty, her eyes as green as the pale pastel of her blouse, a generous mouth, no makeup save for a hint of color on her lips.

"I wonder if you'd do me a favor," she said.

"Be happy to," he answered.

She had caught the inflection of his voice; she said immediately, "You're not American, are you?"

"Yes, I am," he said.

"Small world," she answered, and smiled, and extended her hand. "How do you do?" He took her hand. He could not stop staring at her. Fearing he would embarrass her with his scrutiny, he forced his eyes from her face. Over her shoulder, he saw the man in the brown suit entering the gardens. The newspaper was still folded under his arm. She took her hand from Michael's now. She still had not offered her name, but he did not expect her to, and neither did he offer his.

"This is silly," she said, "but would you mind very much taking a picture of me against the tulips? No one back home will believe I've actually *been* here if I haven't got at least one picture of myself." He could not place her regional dialect, and he was tempted to ask at once what part of the country she was from. Her voice was low-pitched, her speech somewhat mannered and studied. His eyes went to her mouth now, as though he would find the answer there, and again he forced them away. The man with the newspaper was approaching the bench. He did not so much as glance at Michael as he went past. The newspaper was the *Koelner Stadt-Anzeiger*, folded so that the banner and the headline were showing.

"I'm not very good with cameras," Michael said as the man continued up the path. "But if you'll show me how it works . . ."

"It's really very simple," she said. "You focus with the outer ring, and the inner ring takes care of the exposure. You'll see a little circle in there. When the marker is inside the circle, that's it." She shrugged her shoulders at the simplicity of it all.

He accepted the camera and made a great show of studying its mechanism. Actually, he was very good with cameras, was in fact an expert with cameras. Always the lie, he thought.

"Think you've got it?" she asked.

"I hope so," he said. "Shall we try it?"

"Just let me know when," she said.

"Smile," he said, and waited, and then pressed the shutter release button. A tiny *click* sounded on the still sunlit air.

"Thank you," she said. "Now I can go back to shooting more flowers."

"You're very beautiful," he said suddenly.

"Why . . . that's very kind of you," she answered, and slung the camera over her shoulder, waved in farewell, and started up the path. Michael watched as she took another picture further on. She then turned to face him, or rather to face the path that ran past the bench. The viewfinder went up to her eye again. She snapped another picture, waved once more, and then was lost from sight behind a copse of birch trees. He looked again for the man in the brown suit. He was certain this had been Edstrand, he was worried now that the woman's presence might have frightened him away for good. He sat on the bench and waited. The time was almost four-thirty.

The man came into view again not five minutes later. He walked directly to the bench and sat. The two identifying newspapers were now side by side on the bench, between them.

"Michael Henderson?" the man asked.

"Viktor Edstrand?"

"Shall we go through the ritual?" Edstrand asked.

"I suppose we must," Michael said, and smiled.

"The Via Margherita," Edstrand said. "Will that suffice?"

"I've just read *Daisy Miller*," Michael said.

"Very well then."

"What's the trouble?" Michael asked. "They told me on the phone . . ."

"Hans Stolz was killed in Frankfurt on the thirty-first of March," Edstrand said. There was not the slightest trace of emotion in his voice. He might just as easily have been giving Michael a report on the weather. "The police there think it was the work of a burglar. We have heard from West Berlin as well. Helmut Rausch's apartment was ransacked twice in recent weeks."

"And Saalfeld?"

"He is living now in Paris. He appears to be safe. For now."

"What are my instructions?"

"You must go to Berlin at once. If this is what we think it is, we have finally a chance of getting Ernst Koenig."

"I'll make arrangements to leave tonight."

"No, I would not depart abruptly. If you are being watched . . ."

"In the morning then," Michael said. "Who's my contact in Berlin?"

"At the *Walterchens Ballhaus*. Ask for *Gänseblümchen*." Edstrand rose from the bench. He did not offer his hand. "Good luck," he said.

"Thank you."

Michael sat in the sunshine for several moments

more, and then walked off in the opposite direction. Around the bend, past the copse of birch trees, the blond woman was sitting at an outdoor table, sipping tea in the sunshine and looking out over the duck-cluttered lagoon. Impulsively, he walked directly to her table and said, "May I join you?"

"Please," she said, and indicated the vacant chair opposite her.

"I'm Michael Henderson," he said.

"Karin Phillips," she said, and again extended her hand. They shook hands briefly and awkwardly. Out on the lagoon, a pair of mallards were squabbling over some bread a small boy had thrown.

"Are you enjoying your vacation?" he asked.

"Is it that obvious?" she said, and smiled. "I was hoping no one would guess I'm a tourist."

"Actually, you *could* pass for German," he said. "Except for the walk. Besides, I have privileged information."

"Oh?"

"A little while ago, you told me the people back home wouldn't believe . . ."

"Yes, but that doesn't necessarily mean I'm a tourist. I could be an American working in Cologne."

"True. But then you wouldn't be wandering around the gardens at four o'clock on a Tuesday afternoon. The lunch hours are long in Cologne, but not *that* long."

"Ah, but maybe I'm a big executive," she said. "Executives take very long lunch hours."

"If you were an executive in Cologne, you'd have

at least a working knowledge of German. The first thing you asked me was whether I spoke English."

"You're right," she admitted with a smile. "I'm a tourist. And you?"

"I wish I were," he said. "I live in Cologne. I represent an American exporting firm, Bellis Exports. We have a small office in Bonn."

"Where are you from originally?"

"Baltimore," he said. "How about you?"

"Boston."

"Ah, really? What part of Boston?"

"Do you know Boston?"

"I went to school there. B.U."

"Actually, I live just outside of Boston. Brighton, do you know it?"

"Not terribly well," he said. "How long have you been abroad?"

"Since the twelfth. Good Friday. I'm a schoolteacher, we've got a two-week Easter break."

"Then you'll be going back home soon."

"Yes. On the twenty-sixth."

"Where do you go from Cologne?"

"Paris, and then London. What's today's date, anyway?"

"The seventeenth."

"Right. I'm leaving for Paris on the twentieth. Three days there, a few days in London, and then back to the salt mines."

"Did you start the trip here in Cologne?"

"In Zürich. I rented a car there and drove up along the Rhine. It was just lovely."

"Yes," he said. "You don't sound at all Bostonian, you know."

"What you're hearing is the result of thousands of hours of speech classes," she said, and smiled. "That's my subject. Speech and dramatics."

"Then that accounts for it."

"What are *you* doing in the gardens at this time of day?"

"Playing hookey," he said, and glanced at his watch. "Actually, I'd better get back." He hesitated, and then said, "Where are you staying in Cologne?"

"At the *Mondial*. Why?"

"I thought . . . if you're free later, perhaps we could have a drink."

She looked at him for quite a long while before answering. "Well, thank you," she said, "but I think not."

"Some other time maybe," he said.

"Maybe," she said.

He felt suddenly awkward. "Well . . . enjoy the rest of your trip," he said, and rose.

"Thank you."

He walked swiftly from the table. On the lagoon, a duck took sudden wing. He watched its graceful glide, and then left the gardens at the nearest exit. He waited for his trolley, thinking of her. And after he had boarded it, he still thought of her, staring through the window as the car rattled through the city. He could not stop thinking of her. All the way back to the house, he could not shake from his mind that instant when she had kneeled to take a picture, and there had been an intimate glimpse of lace as delicate as all the crushed Aprils he could remember.

Johanna was waiting at the front door of the house they lived in on the *Fraiherr-Vom-Stein-Strasse*. She watched him as he came up the path. They did not embrace at the door.

"Did he arrive?" she asked.

"Yes." Michael looked around the yard. "Where's Lukas?"

"With a friend. We have at least an hour."

"All I need is a minute," Michael said.

"Let's go inside," she said. "You look grave."

Johanna was a German national who still spoke with a faint accent whenever they talked English. This was most of the time; they spoke German only when friends or acquaintances were visiting, and they did not know too many people in Cologne. They had come here together three years ago, after the death of Johanna's husband. Johanna had brought with her an eight-year-old son who'd inherited her dark hair and eyes, her sensuously brooding mouth. Though Lukas had been told repeatedly that Michael was his stepfather, he never called him "Papa." To the young boy, the man with whom he and his mother lived was simply "Michael."

None of their acquaintances thought this significant; Lukas had, after all, lost his father only three years before. Of more interest, to those who speculated about Michael and Johanna, was the fact that the couple rarely seemed to exchange words or gestures of endearment. In fairness, it had to be said that they *did* seem inordinately fond of each other—and yet they behaved more like business partners than man and wife. Never a "*liebchen*," never an intimate pat or embrace, never a loving glance. Ah well, they assumed this was due to Johanna's relatively recent bereavement. It sometimes took a woman years and years to get over her first love. There was a German proverb, *Einmal Witwe, neimals Braut*—"Once a widow, never a bride"—and it seemed to apply here. Besides, most of their friends were certain Michael did not lack for female companionship and affection on his frequent business trips. If this was a marriage of convenience, as many suspected, it seemed comfortable enough nonetheless. Cynically, or perhaps wisely, their few acquaintances in Cologne did not question it too closely; it was best not to pry, *nicht wahr*?

In the living room, he told her briefly of his meeting with Viktor Edstrand. He did not mention his later conversation with the blond American woman. "Stolz was killed in Frankfurt a little more than two weeks ago," he said. "Rausch may be next. I'll be leaving for Berlin in the morning."

"That will seem sudden," she said. "Mathilde may question it."

Mathilde was the girl who worked as secretary for Michael in the small office he maintained in nearby Bonn, some thirty-five kilometers up the Rhine. The name of the company for which he worked was Bellis Exports, Inc., and the home office was located in New

York City—according to the stationery and the notification address inside the front cover of Michael's passport. His name in that passport was Michael Henderson. The passport noted that he had been born in Baltimore, Maryland, on October 12, 1940. It recorded his height as five-feet-eleven-inches, his hair as brown, his eyes as blue. The passport was false, and the export company did not exist. The only true information in the passport was that about his age, his height, and the color of his hair and eyes. But even so short a time as four years ago, the passport he'd carried had shown a photograph of a man with blond hair. And three years before that, he had worn contact lenses, and the color of his eyes had been listed as brown. As for Bellis Exports—

The search for Ernst Koenig had been given the code name "Operation Daisy," and the low-growing European variety of the plant was called *Bellis perennis*. Anything concerning Koenig was linked to the code name "Daisy." In the gardens this afternoon, Edstrand had identified himself by mentioning the Via Margherita in Rome. "*Margherita*" was Italian for daisy. Michael's contact in Berlin was to be someone named "*Gänseblümchen*," and this was German for daisy. One of the major reasons for having moved Michael from Geneva to Cologne three years ago had been information that Koenig was now living here. The information had proved erroneous, but the fake export company had already been labeled Bellis, and the name stuck, even though Michael later became occupied with half-a-dozen projects unrelated to Koenig. In fact, if he had been asked to account for the way he'd spent his time in the past three years, he would have estimated that less than three percent of it had gone to Daisy. But now someone was plucking the petals of the daisy, starting with Stolz in Frankfurt—and suddenly the search was alive again, overshadowing in importance any of his other assignments.

"I'll tell Mathilde someone from the home office is in Berlin and has to see me. She won't pry, Johanna. She's not too terribly bright."

"How long will you be gone?"

"I'm not sure," he said, and rose, and walked to the small bar unit in the corner of the room. "They think Koenig has found them. If so, we have a chance of getting him."

"Are they sure it's Koenig?"

"No. But who else can it be?" He poured two snifters of *Kirschwasser*, and carried both back to the sofa.

"Ah, thank you, Michael," Johanna said.

They sipped at the cherry brandy. The only sound in the living room was the ticking of the large grandfather clock. At last, she said, "Be careful in Berlin."

West Berlin, Germany: April 17, 1974

Helmut Rausch sat waiting in the bar on a side street off *Kurfürsterdamm*. The man who had telephoned him was ten minutes late. The man had identified himself on the phone as an investigator for the Military Police. He had told Rausch the United States Army was interested in his recent burglaries. When Rausch had expressed puzzlement, the man had said simply, in German, "You *work* for the Army, you're a translator for the Army. Naturally, we're concerned." Rausch still could see no connection. He did not translate sensitive material, the burglaries could not possibly be linked to his job with the Army. Besides, the police were *already* investigating, so why was the Army now coming into it?

He was a slender man of fifty-three, wearing a tweed suit, his blond hair combed to hide encroaching baldness, his blue eyes watery and pale. He sat nursing his drink now, waiting for the Army major to arrive. He had been annoyed by the unexpected telephone call, and he was more annoyed now by the major's tardiness. A sudden thought occurred to him—the woman who'd been following him, had she been put on his trail by the Army? He had seen her twice this week, a blond woman wearing a black raincoat. And he was certain he had seen her again not twenty minutes ago, watching him as he'd parked his automobile on the street outside. There had been something vaguely familiar about her face, the high cheek bones, the thin nose and pale eyes—but especially the smile. He realized all at once that she resembled Ernst Koenig, and suddenly his hand began to tremble.

Unbidden, the memory of that day in 1945 returned in a painful rush—the British Second Army approaching Belsen, the frantic haste with which the officers of the camp began destroying papers, destroying evidence. He had been one of three enlisted men in Koenig's unit, and the three had stood by helplessly while the captain did what he said was necessary. And they had obeyed his orders afterwards as well, and had promised to remain silent forever. They had not, of course. They had told all at the trial, and a good thing, too—he was certain their light sentences were directly related to their absolute candor.

He wondered about the girl in the black raincoat again. Her smile had been chilling, it was Koenig's smile exactly. And he wondered, too, if the break-ins at his apartment were somehow linked to the girl, and linked to Koenig as well. His personal belongings, his documents, had been strewn all over the place. He could only conclude that whoever had so invaded his privacy was searching for proof that he was not truly Werner Pollman, a translator for the United States Army, but was instead Helmut Rausch, who had been a German corporal at Belsen in April of 1945.

"Herr Pollman?"

He looked up sharply. The man standing at the table was unmistakably American. He was not in uniform, but this was not unusual. Many soldiers preferred wearing mufti off the base. Was this the major who had called him earlier today?

"Yes?" he answered in English. "I am Werner Pollman."

"Major Avery Hollis," Michael said, and shook

hands with him. He reached into his inside jacket pocket, and produced a plastic-encased identification card. "*Mein Auswais, mein Herr*," he said, and handed the card to Rausch. The card had been prepared for Michael yesterday, by a forger in Cologne. It was printed with the words *Military Police, Criminal Investigation Division*, and below those a picture of Michael, together with the false name and signature. Rausch studied the card without suspicion, and then handed it back to him. As Michael took a chair at the table, he reminded himself again that this man was now Werner Pollman. He had read his dossier from top to bottom more times than he cared to count, and he knew the man's name had once been Helmut Rausch, and yet he could not reveal this knowledge, not yet he couldn't. The irony was not lost on Michael; two men with false identities sitting here in a noisy bar, calling each other Werner Pollman and Avery Hollis; there were, after all, amusing aspects to this whole damn business. The only essential difference between them, he supposed, was that Rausch had *legally* changed his name after his release from prison. As for the rest, they were both liars. In fact, Michael had been lying for so long a time now, he had almost come to believe his own falsehoods. There was a further irony as well. Rausch, or rather Pollman, thought they were there to talk about burglary. Only Michael knew, and could not reveal, that they were there to talk about murder.

"I want to assure you first," he said in German, "that your job is in no way jeopardized by this investigation. We merely want to make certain that the burglaries are not connected with your work at the base."

"I don't see how they could be," Pollman answered in English. His English was in every way superior to Michael's German. He was graciously deferring to Michael now, and perhaps to the United States Army as well, by switching to English. "I've never worked on classified material."

"So I understand. When did the first burglary occur, Herr Pollman?"

"On Easter Sunday. I'd gone to see some friends. When I returned, the entire apartment was in disorder."

"What did the burglar take?"

"Nothing. I thought at first I might have surprised him. He might have heard me coming up the stairs and fled before he could steal anything. But when he came back the second time . . ."

"When was that?"

"Three days ago. When he came back, and again took nothing . . . well, I don't know what to think now."

"Might he have been after any . . . personal documents?"

"Personal documents?" His eyes suddenly narrowed suspiciously. "Why would my personal documents interest a sneak thief?"

"Well," Michael said delicately, "are you . . . you're not involved in an affair of any kind, are you? Someone's wife, or . . ."

"No, no," Pollman said. "No, nothing like that."

"Then there wouldn't be any love letters or . . ."

"No, no, no."

"He wasn't after your passport, was he?" Michael asked. "There's a ready market for passports. Perhaps . . ."

"Well, he did *look* through my passport. But he didn't steal it. He left it in my desk."

"How do you know he looked through it?"

"I had a few five-hundred franc notes tucked between the pages. Swiss francs. I'd forgotten to change them back to marks, and since I frequently go to Switzerland, I simply put them in the passport for later use. Well, the passport was back where it belonged, in one of the desk cubbyholes. But the franc notes were on the floor. So I knew he'd looked through my passport."

"Why do you suppose he did that?"

"I have no idea."

"It seems odd that anyone would look through your passport."

"Yes," Pollman said.

"And he didn't take the franc notes?"

"No."

"Nor any other money?"

"No. There were, oh, perhaps three hundred marks in the top drawer of my dresser. He didn't touch them."

"Herr Pollman, are you *sure* you haven't translated anything for us that might . . . ?"

"Positive."

"Nothing even slightly sensitive?"

"Nothing even *remotely* sensitive. All this week, I've been translating invoices from meat packers, for example. You have no idea how much meat the American Army eats."

"And the week before that?"

"Major Hollis, please let me assure you that my work at the base is routine. The burglaries cannot possibly be related to it."

"Mm," Michael said, and paused, seemingly thinking about what he might ask next, even though he knew *exactly* what he would ask next. It was the single most important question he had come here to ask. "Prior to the burglaries," he said, "were there any threatening letters or telephone calls from anyone?"

"None."

"From someone in your past, perhaps? Someone who might be bearing a grudge?"

"My past?" Pollman said. His eyes narrowed again. "What do you mean, my past?"

"Past business associates? Or friends? Anything like that?"

"No."

"And I don't suppose *you've* threatened anyone recently," Michael said, and smiled. "You haven't written to anyone . . ."

"No. Threaten? I'm not sure I understand you. Why would I threaten anyone?"

"Just a thought," Michael said. A thought indeed, he thought. The *only* damn thought he had about the whole thing. If none of the three were threatening Koenig, why had he resurfaced after all these years of hiding? Why was he now out to eliminate them?

Pollman looked suddenly into his face, as though unexpected scrutiny would guarantee a truthful answer. "Am I being followed, Major Hollis?" he asked. "Has the Army assigned someone to follow me?"

"No," Michael said, and then immediately, "*Has* someone been following you?"

"I think so. Yes, I'm fairly certain."

"Who? Can you describe him to me?"

"It's not a man. It's a woman."

"What does she look like?"

"A young woman, certainly no older than twenty-eight or twenty-nine. Blond hair, light eyes. I've seen her three times now. She was wearing a black raincoat each time."

"When's the last time you saw her?"

"Just before I came in here. As I was parking the car." He shook his head. "It may have been my imagination. This whole business has made me very nervous."

"Herr Pollman, when your apartment was broken into . . . you didn't find any lipsticked cigarette ends on the floor or in the ashtrays, did you? You didn't smell perfume or powder when you unlocked the door?"

"No, not that I can remember. Anyway, I frequently have women in my apartment. Such things would not have seemed unusual to me."

"But you say a woman has been following you."

"Yes."

"Has she ever approached you?"

"No. I know exactly what you're thinking. I thought the same thing at first. But she's not a prostitute, she doesn't look like a prostitute. Besides, in this city, the prostitutes aren't so shy." He looked at his watch. "Major Hollis," he said, "if we're finished here, I have another appointment. I hope you'll excuse me."

"Yes, certainly," Michael said. "I appreciate the time you've given me."

He paid for Pollman's drink, and together they walked outside. On the sidewalk, in the gathering dusk, Pollman asked, "May I give you a ride, Major?"

"Thank you, no," Michael said. "I think I'll stroll a bit." He intended to hail a taxi and follow Pollman's car. If Pollman had a female follower, the follower was now about to acquire a follower of her own. He watched as Pollman walked to the small car parked at the curb, watched as he unlocked the door and climbed inside. He saw Pollman reaching over to the glove box, taking a pair of driving gloves from it, and pulling them onto his hands. He saw Pollman inserting a key into the ignition switch. He saw Pollman twisting the key.

The explosion tore open the separating wall between the rear engine and the back seat, engulfed the entire machine in flames, and hurled Werner Pollman or rather Helmut Rausch, through the front windshield—dead.

Cologne, Germany: April 20, 1974

They met again in the gardens. Edstrand was wearing a dark blue suit this time. They dispensed with the formality of identification. They knew each other this time, or knew each other as well as anyone in this business ever got to know anyone.

"What have you got for me?" Michael asked.

"Nothing. You did not give us very much to go on."

"I didn't *have* very much to go on."

"Even so. A blond woman, twenty-eight, twenty-nine years of age. Light eyes." Edstrand shook his head. "We cannot work miracles. There are perhaps twenty million women in the world who would fit that description."

"Yes, but not all of them are going around doing Koenig's dirty work."

"You cannot be sure of that, Henderson. You do not know the woman is working for Koenig. There may be no connection whatever."

"Then why was she following Rausch?"

Edstrand shrugged.

"What does Berlin have to say about her?" Michael asked.

"Berlin has nothing on her."

"And Frankfurt?"

"Nothing. We are checking again Koenig's dossier. Perhaps there is some clue there. In the meantime, you are wasting time here in Cologne. We want you to go to Paris at once. It is time to confront Saalfeld. As *himself*."

"Who made *that* brilliant decision?" Michael asked.

"It was made, I do not know who made it."

"I don't see that it'll accomplish a damn thing."

"You are becoming edgy," Edstrand said.

"Yes, two people have been killed, I'm becoming edgy, yes. I make a simple request for information . . ."

"It is not a simple request. And besides, we are still working on it."

"She's the only possible lead we have to Koenig . . ."

"We are working on it."

"What am I supposed to tell Saalfeld?"

"That we know who he is. That we have known all along."

"Why?"

"There is no longer need for caution. We have been watching those three for years now, and never has Koenig made a move against them in reprisal. We thought he would attempt to retaliate after the trial. But no. So we have waited. And now two of them are dead. We must warn Saalfeld, we must openly enlist his aid. The truth will be best now."

"When do you want me to leave?"

"There is a plane at 1905, it arrives in Paris at 2010. Your passage has been booked." He reached into his pocket, took from it a small notebook and a pen, and scrawled a name and telephone number on one of the pages. He tore the page from the book. "If you need help in Paris, these are the people to contact," he said. "They have been watching Saalfeld."

Michael looked at the page Edstrand handed to him. The name on it was Marguerite Deveaux. "Marguerite" was French for daisy.

"Don't you think we're beginning to run this 'daisy' thing into the ground?" Michael asked.

"Eh?" Edstrand said. "Oh, Marguerite you mean. That happens to be her real name," he said, and shrugged.

Michael folded the page and put it into his wallet. "If there's anything on the blond woman . . ."

"We will let you know."

"Is that it then?" Michael asked.

"I can think of nothing else," Edstrand answered.

Cologne, Germany to Paris, France: April 20, 1974

The plane left Cologne five minutes late. As soon as they were airborne, Michael asked the stewardess for a copy of *Paris-Soir*. He had not been in France for close to six months; he feared his French would be rusty, and he knew of no better way to brush up on it. At twenty minutes to eight, a half-hour before the plane was scheduled to land at Orly Airport, Karin Phillips took the vacant seat beside him. He had not seen her at the Cologne Airport, had not noticed her boarding the plane, and was surprised to see her now. And a trifle embarrassed. He did not ordinarily try to pick up strangers in public gardens, and her rejection had reminded him of those clumsy days of his adolescence, when crossing a high-school gymnasium to ask a girl to dance was something close to Chinese torture.

"Hello," she said, and smiled. "Small world."

"Small world indeed."

"You always seem to have a newspaper," she said.

"You always seem to have a camera."

"I've been watching you. You're a lip reader."

"Only when I'm reading French."

"How have you been?"

"Fine."

"*Where* have you been?" she said.

"Out of town," he said. "On business." And suddenly wondered how she'd known he'd been away.

"I looked for you," she said. "I went back to the gardens. I thought you might be playing hookey again."

"Why'd you look for me?"

"I had a present for you."

"I'll accept it now," he said, and smiled.

"Sorry, it's packed in one of my valises."

"What sort of present is it?"

"A picture. The one I took of you in the gardens."

"I didn't realize you'd taken my picture," he said.

"Oh, yes. When I turned back, remember?"

"I thought you were taking a long shot of the path."

"No. It was you."

"Why'd you take a picture of me?"

"Oh, I don't know," she said, and shrugged. "Anyway, I went back. But you weren't there."

"I was in Berlin."

"How's every little thing in Berlin?" she said.

"Fine."

"I meant to get there," she said, "but now it's too late."

"That's right, this *is* the twentieth, isn't it? Three days in Paris, a few in London, and then back to the salt mines."

"You have a good memory."

"Where are you staying in Paris?" he asked.

"At the *Meurice*. It's expensive, but what the hell."

"I'll be at the *Mont-Thabor*," he said. "Maybe we'll run into each other."

"Maybe," she answered.

He had not once mentioned Johanna, and he did not mention her for the rest of the flight. At Orly, he helped her gather her luggage, and then found a taxi for her. She rolled down the window and offered her hand in farewell. He took it—and felt compelled to cling to it. A warning signal flashed, but he ignored it; he was not going to let her out of his life now that she had entered it again.

"Karin," he said, "would you like to have dinner with me tonight?"

She seemed surprised by his invitation. She did not answer.

"I won't be free till about ten," he said. "But they dine late in Paris."

Still she did not answer.

"Well," he said, and shrugged.

"I'd love to, Michael," she said.

"The *Meurice* then," he said. "Ten o'clock."

"I'll be waiting," she answered, and gently took her hand from his.

He watched the taxi as it pulled away from the curb. His heart was pounding. He did not know whether he was frightened or merely in love.

Paris, France: April 20, 1974

It was bitterly cold for this late in April.

The sky above was black and unremitting, the night impaled on a bayonet wind that crunched through bone and drained the spirit. Michael had parked the rented automobile two city blocks from Saalfeld's apartment, and then had stepped out of the car into the wind's fierce attack. There appeared to be no point of origin for each moaning gust, nor any defense against the fury that swept indiscriminately from the rooftops. The two blocks to Saalfeld's apartment might have been two hundred.

A brass escutcheon outside the street-level apartment was etched with the name *Georges Lédard*. Michael pressed the bell button and heard chimes sounding somewhere within. He waited. He heard footsteps approaching the oversized wooden doors. A maid in a black uniform peered out at him.

"*Oui, monsieur*?" she asked.

"*Monsieur Lédard, s'il vous plait.*"

She must have detected his accent, for she said at once in English, "May I say who is calling, please?"

"Mr. Henderson. It concerns Rudolph Saalfeld."

"*Un moment*," she said, and gently closed the door again. She returned several minutes later, and led Michael through a high vaulted entrance foyer and into an ornately decorated drawing room. The man standing before the fireplace was in his late fifties, with graying hair and an expansive middle. His nose could have been French. His eyes were blue. His posture, despite the paunch, was quite erect.

"I'm afraid I do not know you," he said in English.

"I know you don't," Michael answered.

"Nor this Mr. Saalberg to whom you referred."

"Saal*feld*," Michael corrected. "Would you mind very much if I closed these doors?" He did not wait for an answer. He went immediately to the doors, closed them, and then twisted the key in the big brass lock. Turning from the doors, he said, "Stolz and Rausch are dead."

"Stolz? Rausch? I do not know these names."

"I think you know them, sir."

"I'm sorry, I do not."

"They were with you at Belsen in the spring of 1945."

"Belsen? I have never been to Germany in my life."

"You were *born* in Germany," Michael said. "In 1945, you were serving with the German Army as a sergeant. And you were attached to the concentration camp at Belsen. Your name then was Rudolph Saalfeld."

"Mr. Henderson, really . . ."

"I'd appreciate it if we could talk candidly," Michael said. "Your life is in danger."

"How is it in danger?"

"I just told you. Stolz and Rausch have been killed."

"You did not say they'd been killed," he said, and sighed. "You only said they were dead."

"May we talk honestly now?"

"I have not been Rudolph Saalfeld for a long time," he said, and sighed again. "Why do you bother me now? I served my prison sentence, I paid my debt . . ."

"Koenig hasn't. He's wanted for murder."

"I don't *care* about Koenig!"

"We do. We want to bring him to trial, Herr Saalfeld. In 1945, he killed a man. Now that may not seem too terribly important to you, the death of a single man when so *many* lives were being taken. But if we value our own humanity at all, Herr Saalfeld, it *becomes* important. We want to find Koenig. We want him to pay for his crime."

Saalfeld went to an easy chair near the fireplace and sank heavily into it. "What do you want to know?" he asked.

"According to your testimony at the trial . . ."

"*Must* we go over all of this again?"

"Yes, I'm sorry but I think we must. At the trial you said that you and the others were in a unit commanded by Captain Ernst Koenig. Your *job*, as you put it, was to take from prisoners entering the camp anything of value on their persons—rings, watches, bracelets, necklaces, and the like."

"Yes," Saalfeld said, and rose abruptly. "I would like a drink. Would you care for something to drink?"

"No, thank you."

"I would like a drink," he said again, and went to a wall panel, which he pressed with the palm of his hand, revealing a bar behind it. Quickly, he poured himself a cognac.

"You further testified," Michael said, "that the loot obtained from the prisoners was regularly sent to the *Reichsbank* in Berlin, on the fifteenth of each month."

"That is correct. We packed the jewelry into crates, and it was sent via military convoy to the *Reichsbank*."

"Where it was melted into ingots, and then stored in the underground vaults there."

"Yes, that is all true."

"All right," Michael said, and nodded. "In April of 1945, when the British were approaching Belsen, Captain Koenig panicked. According to your testimony, he shot one of the prisoners in cold blood, and then put *his* uniform and *his* identification papers on the dead man. At gunpoint, he forced you and the other men in the unit—Rausch and Stolz—to carry a crate of confiscated gold jewelry out to a waiting weapons carrier. Before he drove away from the camp, he swore you to silence, and then said—and please correct me if I'm wrong—'Captain Koenig is dead. Remember that.' "

"*Ja*," Saalfeld said, reverting to German. "*Kapitän Koenig ist tot*. But at the trial, I told them he was still alive. I told them that."

"Yes. You told them that."

"Anyway, it is over and done with," Saalfeld said. "I served my prison term. I changed my name when I was released. I moved to Paris and started a new life. It is all over and done with. What do you want from me now?"

"I want to know why, after all this time, Koenig now feels the three of you are a danger to him."

"Do you know for certain that he is the one who killed Stolz and Rausch?"

"Not for certain, no."

"Then . . ."

"Have you had any contact at all with him since that day in 1945?"

"None."

"You've never corresponded with him?"

"Never. I do not know where he is. I have no desire to know where he is."

"Have you kept in touch with Stolz and Rausch?"

"No. This is the first I am hearing of them since the trial."

"Then you wouldn't know whether one of *them* might have written to Koenig, or . . ."

"I have no idea."

"At the trial you said you didn't remember the name of the prisoner Koenig shot. The man with whom he later exchanged clothes and papers. Would you happen to remember that name now?"

"No. He was new at the camp, that's all I remember. None of the other prisoners knew him, he had only arrived that morning. I think that is why Koenig selected him. The man was, in effect, anonymous. And also, he resembled Koenig somewhat. In size, do you know, and in coloring. Blond, do you know? Like Koenig himself. It was not a random choice."

"Are you sure you don't remember the man's name?"

"I am positive."

"When I spoke to Rausch in Berlin, he told me he was being followed by a blond woman. Are *you* being followed as well?"

"Not that I know of."

"You've seen no blond woman?"

"I've seen many blond women. There are many blond women in Paris. But none of them are following me. More's the pity," he said, and smiled ruefully.

"I don't think I've impressed upon you the seriousness of the situation," Michael said. "If Koenig . . ."

"You have indeed sufficiently warned me," Saalfeld said. "But I must tell you, Mr. Henderson, if a man forgets how to smile, he also forgets how to live. Do you not find it amusing that a person I scarcely knew may now want to kill me? I was at the camp for only six months. I knew Koenig solely as my commanding officer."

"What kind of officer was he?"

"I met worse in the Army, and also better," Saalfeld said, and shrugged. "He was never cruel to the men in his command. I know he shot a prisoner, I am still appalled by what he did. But in fairness, I must say he treated us well. In fact, he treated us kindly."

"In what way."

"Oh, little things. I remember once, he brought back a bottle of *Schnapps* from the village for us. And another time, it was Christmas, the war was beginning to go badly and none of us were permitted home for the holiday. But he allowed us to have a little party there at the camp. He was kind to us in many ways. One night, I remember, we had been drinking in the village and were making our way back to the camp, walking along the road to the camp, you know. And Captain Koenig was in the village too that night, and he was driving his woman home. He stopped the car for us. He did not have to give us a ride back to the camp, but he did. Little kindnesses like . . ."

"His woman?" Michael said. "What woman?"

"His woman in the village."

"What was her name?"

"I don't remember. He was living with her, oh, for many months. Long before I was assigned to the camp."

"What did she look like, do you remember?"

"Oh yes, we would see her with him quite often. She was a good-looking woman, a trim figure, a very pretty face. She was mad for him . . . well, he was a very handsome man, you know."

"*H*ow old was she?"

"Twenty? Twenty-one? Certainly no older. We used

to call her *Die Schönheit*. That means 'The Beauty' in German."

"Can you describe her more completely?" Michael asked. "What color was her hair?"

"Brown, I think. Yes, brown."

"And her eyes?"

"Blue. Like the captain's."

"And you have no idea what her name was?"

"No, I'm sorry. Her father was . . . what? A baker? A pastry chef? I'm not sure. It was very long ago." His voice lowered. "There were rumors that she was pregnant by the captain. But that may only have been barracks talk."

In his hotel room, Michael took from his wallet the number Edstrand had given him, and dialed it. A woman answered the phone.

"*Allo*," she said.

"Marguerite Deveaux, please," Michael said.

"This is she."

"This is Michael Henderson of Bellis Exports," he said. "I was told to contact you if I needed any assistance in Paris. I'll be leaving the hotel in about forty minutes, but I'd like to talk to you before then. Would it be possible for you to come here?"

"*Bien sûr, monsieur*," she said. "What hotel are you at?"

"The *Mont-Thabor*."

"I shall be there," she said, and hung up.

He jiggled the receiver bar, and when he got the hotel operator, he told her he wished to place a call to Cologne, Germany, and gave her the number of his home phone. She told him she would get back to him. He had already showered and shaved, and was partially dressed when the telephone rang. He immediately lifted the receiver from its cradle.

"Hello?" he said.

"Ready on your call now, monsieur," the operator said. He waited. Johanna's voice came onto the line.

"Michael?" she said. "How are you?"

"Fine, thanks. Johanna, I hate to bother you with business at this hour, but I've talked to the Bellis attorney here in Paris, and he needs more figures."

"Yes, Michael," she said. "What figures does he need?"

"Are you familiar with the files on Regal Novelty?"

In German, "regal" was "*königlich.*" Johanna instantly knew he was referring to Ernst Koenig. "Yes," she said, "what about it?"

"Apparently a woman in Belsen was closely related with the firm several years back, before it went bankrupt. We'd like to locate her now because she was familiar with the entire operation, and might be a material witness in our lawsuit. But we can't locate her name in any of the files. In fact, all we've got is a description of her. I wonder if you can put the home office on it."

"I'll try to help," Johanna said. "What description do you have?"

"The woman would have been about twenty or twenty-one at the time, brown hair and blue eyes, trim figure, pretty. Our records indicate her father was either a baker or a pastry chef in Belsen, but they may be inaccurate."

"How close was her relationship with Regal?"

"She was intimately involved, from what I understand. In fact, there's speculation that Regal was the parent company of a smaller firm she started."

"There's nothing about that in the files," Johanna said. "No indication that Regal ever merged with another company."

"This wouldn't have been an official merger, Johanna. But if any stock was issued, we ought to know about it, don't you think?"

"Most definitely," she said.

"Will you get back to me as soon as you can?"

"I'll contact the home office immediately," she said.

"Thank you. Give my love to Lukas."

"I will. And mine to Daisy," she said, and hung up.

He was knotting his tie when the telephone rang again. He lifted the receiver. "Hello?"

"Monsieur Henderson?"

"Yes?"

"Marguerite Deveaux. I am downstairs in the lobby."

"Please come up," he said. "It's Room 412."

Marguerite Deveaux was a woman in her late forties. She was wearing a dark brown overcoat, which she did not remove. She sat heavily in a chair facing the door, as though expecting imminent intrusion; he had always found the French overly cautious.

"So," she said, "how may we assist?"

"Two things," Michael said. "First, when I spoke to Rausch in Berlin, he told me he thought he was being followed. Have any of . . . ?"

"By our people there, do you mean?"

"No. By a blond woman. In a black raincoat."

"Oh my," Marguerite said, and giggled unexpectedly. "*Comme une espionne du cinéma, n'est-ce pas*? A cinema spy." She shook her head in disbelief. "I have met many agents in my lifetime," she said, "from since the war, whan I was with the underground. But a blonde in a black raincoat?" She giggled again. "That is good Hitchcock, but it is bad espionage."

"I take it you haven't seen her in Paris."

"If she is here, none of our people have mentioned her in their reports."

"Rausch seemed pretty certain about her."

"We will watch, of course. What is the second thing?"

"What are the chances of getting Saalfeld out of Paris?"

"How do you mean?"

"If we asked him to leave, would he?"

"I do not know the man personally, but we have been watching him a long time, and he is a creature of habit, eh? *Il vit dans un monde d'habitude, comprenez*? He owns an architectural firm in Lagny sur Marne, he arrives there promptly at eight each morning, eats his lunch each day at noon, returns to the office at two-thirty, and then goes home at seven each night. He takes a holiday once each year, in August, when all the Frenchmen go. A man of routine, of schedule. I do not think we could convince him to leave now, in April."

"Even though he knows Koenig is after him?"

"But he has *always* known this, *n'est-ce pas*? Why else did he change his name after he was released from prison? Who even *cared* that he had once been an unimportant sergeant at Belsen? Who except Koenig? *Non*. I do not think he will leave Paris voluntarily."

"Could we take him by force?"

"*Mais, oui*, we can do anything by force. But for that, we need instructions from a higher authority."

"How high? Edstrand?"

"Higher than that. Why do you want him out of Paris?"

"Paris is too big. If Koenig is here . . ."

"Or the woman in the black raincoat, eh?" Marguerite said, and again giggled. It seemed to Michael she was enjoying the joke far too extravagantly. She sensed his annoyance, and sobered immediately. "Of course, I understand your point. He would be easier to contain elsewhere. Here, he could be shot in broad daylight on the *Champs-Élysées*, and his murderer would be lost in minutes. Where did you have in mind?"

"Someplace very small and very exclusive, where we could watch him day and night."

"Someplace like Devil's Island, eh?" she said, and smiled. "It is certainly very small and exclusive. *Trés chic, aussi*," she added dryly. "Anyway, there are many places; I can think of a hundred in France alone. *If* they agree it is to be done. Do you wish me to inquire?"

"Please."

"I shall do so tonight. Was there anything else?"

"Not for now."

"Then I will telephone you in the morning. *Au 'voir, monsieur.*"

He became suspicious during dinner.

In the gardens that morning, Edstrand had said, "A blond woman, twenty-eight, twenty-nine years of age. Light eyes. There are perhaps twenty million women in the world who would fit that description."

The woman sitting opposite him was a blond with pale green eyes. He had estimated her age at twenty-nine or thirty. She had told him she was Karin Phillips, a schoolteacher on vacation from Brighton, Massachusetts. But just a few moments ago, she said something that caused him to wonder whether that, *too*, was a lie.

They had been talking about the Rhine Valley, where she had spent the better part of her vacation thus far, and she had mentioned that her favorite castle had been Eltz, just outside Koblenz. He had explained that Eltz was really *four* castles in one, what the Germans called an *Ahnerbenhaus*. In days of yore, he had said (He had actually heard himself saying "In days of yore") four related families had banded together to share a common stronghold, and Eltz was the result.

"Must have cut expenses a lot," Karin had said, and laughed.

"Capitalists living communistically," Michael had said.

"I think I'd prefer my own little *schloss*, though," Karin had said. "Give me Charlottenburg, and let the other three families fend for themselves."

He had heard the remark, but it had not registered immediately. Or perhaps he had simply chosen to ignore it. He had gone on a bit more about Eltz, telling her his favorite inscription in the castle was the one on a baroque clay stove dating back to 1650, "*Mars stands for sorrow. Peace brings joy and a happy morrow*," and then they had begun talking about the happy coincidence of being on the same flight from Cologne to Paris, and suddenly he remembered a snatch of conversation from the plane:

"*How's every little thing in Berlin?*"

"*Fine.*"

"*I meant to get there, but now it's too late.*"

And just as suddenly, Karin Phillips became suspect. He told himself he was being foolish—stay in this business long enough and eventually you began to distrust your own mother. But the fact remained that Charlottenburg was a castle in *Berlin*; it had been the favorite home of Queen Sophie-Charlotte, the wife of Friedrich I. Karin had not been to Berlin, yet she had just made easy reference to a castle she could not have seen *except* in Berlin.

"I meant to ask," he said. "Is this your first trip abroad?"

"Yes," she said. "I thought you knew."

He debated whether he should question her further; was the Charlottenburg remark far enough behind them? He decided to risk it.

"It's a pity you didn't get to Berlin," he said. "Maybe next time."

Her wine glass hesitated on the way to her lips. The pause was imperceptible, she recovered almost immediately. He watched her eyes and her hands. Whatever she said next would make no difference at all. If she knew she'd made a mistake, she would now try to cover it, and her words would undoubtably be effective. Only the eyes and the hands would tell him what he wanted to know. "Actually, I've read so much about Berlin, I almost feel I've been there," she said. Nothing flickered in her eyes, there was no indication of mental backtracking. "Do you know how high the *Funkturm* is, for example?"

"I have no idea," he said.

"Four hundred and fifty-two feet," she said, "and it's known to Berliners as 'The Lump.' Or did you know that the equestrian statue in the courtyard at Charlottenburg was sculpted by Andreas Schlüter in 1703?"

"Yes, that I knew."

"Then you must've read the same guidebook I did," she said, and laughed. "Who *was* Andreas Schlüter, anyway?"

Her hands were still steady, she sipped slowly at her wine. His own wine had gone sour. They sat opposite each other at a table overlooking the Seine, and in the distance he could see the lighted towers of Notre Dame, and he wondered now when he had last looked into anyone's eyes without searching for a lie there. In his youth, he had been taught to trust people. His father had owned and operated a hardware store in Vermont, and he'd sometimes let debts go by for months at a time, secure in the knowledge that his friends and neighbors would pay him when they could. He had passed on this sense of trust to Michael, and it had been fortified by Michael's mother, who placed her ultimate trust in God. He wondered now how he had come so far from home in so short a time. When had the erosion begun? Not in college certainly, not then. He had written home in his sophomore year—his father was dead by then, his mother was living with her sister in New Hampshire—he had told her he wanted to become a doctor; "I want to heal people," he had written in his almost illegible scrawl. Nor had the Army done anything to weaken the beliefs his parents had instilled in him. If anything, he learned on the Korean battlefield the absolute necessity of trusting the man who stood beside you in the bitter cold, fighting a common enemy. It was later, perhaps, when he was transferred to Intelligence and put to work as a cryptographer, that he first began to feel he was doing something less than honorable. Deciphering codes was like reading someone's personal mail. And though the "someone" was still the enemy, he felt tainted by the job, and became even more determined to go on to medical school when he was discharged. He thought he might become a surgeon; he had seen the miracles performed by surgeons in the heat of battle. Back at school, he'd begun to drift. His grades dropped—he was especially weak in his science courses—and he began to doubt he'd ever be admitted to any decent medical school. The war had done something to him; war—*any* war—always did something to a man.

He was first approached by a recruiter in Canada, where he'd gone to spend a weekend with a girl whose name he could no longer remember. The man introduced himself as Henry Lefferts—he now knew the name was a false one—and he told Michael they'd been impressed by his work with code while he'd been in the Army, and suggested that perhaps he might be interested in civilian espionage work. It had sounded glamorous at the time. Espionage. Very glamorous. He began by working code, but only for a very short time before he was assigned to one of the banana republics where a *coup* was expected. From there, he had been sent to the Middle East, and then to Japan, then . . . he could no longer remember the succession of events or places that finally brought him to Germany. He remembered only that somewhere back beyond the furthest reaches of his memory, there had once been a young man who'd wanted to become a physician. And somehow, that young man had . . .

"*Do* you know?" she said.

"I'm sorry, do I know what?"

"Who Andreas Schlüter was?"

"No, I don't."

It was entirely possible that she *had* learned of Charlottenburg from the guidebooks. In which case, all was coincidence. Coincidentally, she had been in the Cologne gardens on the day he'd learned of Stolz's death, and had taken a photograph of him which she'd already had developed, even though she was still on vacation. Had she taken a picture of Edstrand as well? For what purpose? Identification of the enemy? And coincidentally, she had been on the same plane from Cologne to Paris tonight, which was after all quite possible since there were only two flights daily, one in the morning and the other at night, which made the odds fifty-fifty. And after all, she *had* told him she'd be leaving for Paris on the twentieth, and this *was* the twentieth, so there was nothing surprising about finding her on that airplane, nothing surprising about the fact that she was now sitting across from him as the lights of *Notre Dame* blazed in the distance.

But Rausch had been killed in Berlin on the seventeenth, he had started his automobile and been blown to smithereens not ten minutes after he'd told Michael he was being followed by a blonde, had indeed said he'd *seen* the blonde outside while he was parking his car. And now Karin Phillips knew all about Charlottenburg in Berlin, and of course she had only got the information from the same guidebook that had told her the Radio Tower was 452 feet high. All coincidence. But Michael knew there was no such thing as coincidence in this business.

"Tell me about yourself," he said. "All I know is

that you're a schoolteacher from Brighton. Where in Brighton?"

"If you don't know Brighton . . ."

"I know it," he lied. "I once dated a girl from there."

"Ah. Well then, do you know Commonwealth Terrace?"

"Yes."

"That's where I live. In a white house with yellow shutters."

"And where do you teach?"

"At a private school called Hopewell Academy."

"I don't know it."

"It's relatively new," she said. "It used to be an all-girls' school—the Grace Hopewell School. The name was changed in 1967, when they began admitting boys."

"What do you do besides teach?" he asked.

"Well, that takes up a good deal of my time, you know. But I . . . well, let me see . . . my hobbies, do you mean?"

"Yes."

"I enjoy taking pictures, as you know. And I play tennis, and swim, and in the winter I ski a lot . . ."

"Where?"

"In Vermont, usually."

"Where in Vermont?"

"Stowe. Sugarbush." She shrugged. "Wherever there's snow."

"Are you married? Engaged? Serious about anyone?"

"No. How about you? Are you married?"

"No," he said, and turned away from the table to signal the wine steward.

"Or engaged? Or serious about anyone?"

"None of those," he said.

"*Oui, monsieur*?" the wine steward said.

"*C'était magnifique, ce vin-ci*," Michael said. "*Encore une bouteille, s'il vous plait*."

"Couldn't we get a half-bottle instead?" she asked Michael, and then said to the waiter, in fluent French, "*N' est-ce pas possible d'avoir une demi-bouteille de ce vin*?"

"*Comme vous voulez, mademoiselle*," he replied.

"Would that be all right, Michael? A half-bottle?"

"Certainly," Michael said, and nodded to the steward, who left the table immediately. "Your French is very good," he said.

"Thank you."

"Where'd you learn it?"

"In college."

"Where was that?"

"The University of Wisconsin."

"Where you also majored in speech and dramat ics."

"Yes, and minored in education."

"Do you enjoy teaching?"

"Not very much. Shall I tell you a secret?"

"Please."

"I really wanted to be an actress. Went through the whole experience, moved to New York, lived in a rat-infested apartment on West Forty-eighth, made the rounds, ever hopeful." She rolled her eyes. "Well, when you get to be twenty-five, and you're still a hopeful ingenue without a job, it's time to reconsider, don't you think? I began teaching three years ago."

"But you don't like it."

"I've often thought of quitting. Especially on this trip. Driving up the Rhine, I even entertained the ridiculous notion of never going back to the States. Do you think anyone in Europe might be talked into hiring a former private schoolteacher from Brighton, Massachusetts?"

"I'd hire you tomorrow," he said honestly, and almost forgot that not five minutes ago he had doubted her credentials. What the hell was the matter with him? The girl was exactly who and what she said she was. Or had she simply learned a role as well as he had learned his own? Had a fabricated past become so merged with the present that she could reconstruct it without effort and present it as fact—and perhaps even believe it herself? He longed in that moment to tell her the absolute truth about himself, tell her that Michael Henderson was only the most recent in a long line of aliases he had used since becoming an agent. Agent. The polite synonym for spy. Spy. The glamorous euphemism for fake, liar, cheat, and occasional assassin. "Do you know who I am?" he thought. I am not Michael Henderson, I am not that man for sure, whoever he may be. I was *not* born in Baltimore, Maryland, I did *not* go to college in Boston, my wife and stepson in Cologne . . .

"Enough about me," she said. "Now tell me about *you*."

And he told her all the lies.

And later, in the taxi on the way back to her hotel, he kissed her. Breathlessly, they moved apart from each other, and stared into each other's faces. The lights of Paris flashed past the taxicab windows. The wind had died, the fountains threw open, multicolored petals of water into the night.

"Be careful," she whispered.

"Why?"

"I may *never* go home."

"Stay," he said. "Never go home."

"Don't tempt me."

"Be tempted."

He kissed her again. He thought briefly of Johanna. How could he ever explain Johanna to her? They were almost at the hotel, the taxi had crossed the bridge on *Boulevard St. Michel*, and was turning onto *Rue Rivoli*. For a frightening moment, he thought he would lose her the moment he surrendered her to the massive stone anonymity of the hotel.

"Will I see you tomorrow?" he asked.

"I'm . . . not sure. I feel terribly confused all at once."

"Shall I call you?"

"Let me call you. I know where you're staying."

"Karin . . ."

"Michael, please. I have to . . . think about this. Decisions aren't easy for me. I agonized for months before taking the teaching job. If I'm to stay in Europe now . . ."

"Are you seriously considering it?"

"Yes," she said, "I'm seriously considering it." She touched his lips with her hand. "Does that frighten you?"

"Yes," he admitted.

"Me, too."

The taxi pulled up in front of the hotel. Michael came around to the curbside, opened the door for her, and then paid the driver. The driver studied the tip as though it were contaminated. In fluent French, Michael told him that the tip was more than adequate, and if the driver considered it unfair, he could simply return the money to Michael who would find far better use for it. The driver immediately said he was not questioning the tip, *monsieur*, in fact, the tip was exceedingly generous. Walking into the lobby, Michael realized he had not caused even such a minor scene in as long as he could remember. In his business, obscurity was a virtue. You did not argue with waiters or taxicab drivers, you tried to remain as anonymous as possible, you blended into the landscape, you lost yourself. With Karin Phillips, he had found himself again.

At the elevators, he kissed her briefly and discreetly on the cheek. The French, for all their reputation as lovers, frowned upon liaisons in their chaste hotels.

"I'll call you tomorrow," he said.

"I'll be sightseeing," she answered. "And thinking. But I *will* call you, I promise."

"I'll be waiting."

"I may surprise you," she said.

"How?"

"I may tell you I love you and want to spend the rest of my life with you."

"Tell me now."

The elevator arrived. She stepped into it, and blew a kiss at him just before the doors closed.

He wore the wafted kiss like a flower in his lapel, and when he reached his own hotel, the *concierge* looked at him in amazement, as though this foolishly grinning American could not possibly be the same sober-faced and businesslike man who had left here not three hours before.

Lagny-sur-Marne, France: April 21, 1974

They had succeeded in frightening him, that much they had done. On the half-hour drive from Paris to the suburb of Lagny, Saalfeld narrowly studied every automobile with a blond woman at the wheel. He had not realized there were so many blondes in Paris. He had told the American that there were many blondes here, but *this* many? It seemed to him now that half the women in Paris had bleached their hair overnight. By the time he reached his office, he was drenched with perspiration. He did something he had never done in his life. At eight in the morning, he took a bottle of cognac from where it was hidden in the bottom drawer of his desk, and poured himself a snifter-full. He did not linger over the drink. He gulped it down hastily, and then returned bottle and unwashed snifter to the drawer.

It was a magnificent day, the breezes gentle and balmy in contrast to the high winds that had lashed Paris the night before. A man had no right to be afraid of anything on a day as lovely as today. And yet he was afraid. From the mullioned terrace doors in his office, he could see the parklike grounds surrounding his offices. He had worked long and hard to build this firm. He had come to France with a new name and no education to speak of. He had studied the language until he could speak it like a native, though not without a trace of German accent. To those who queried this, he said that he was originally from Alsace. Georges Lédard, he was, and as Georges Lédard he had entered architectural school, the oldest student in the class, and the one who was graduated with the highest honors. He apprenticed himself to other men in the beginning, but he had diligently saved his money till he felt he could risk starting his own company. *Lédard & Cie., Architectes.* That was what the large sign at the entrance to the grounds said. And now, was all this to be negated by a man he had not seen for twenty-nine years? Was he himself to be eliminated as easily as had the unfortunate victim at Belsen?

At ten A.M., the intercom on his desk sounded. He pressed a button in the base, and said, "Yes?"

"A Sister Thérèse Falgueirettes to see you," his secretary said.

"*Pardon?*"

"She is a nun, Monsieur Lédard. From a convent near Compiègne. They are rebuilding one of the wings, and are in need of architectural assistance. Something to do with buttressing the old walls."

"Very well, show her in," he said, and sighed.

Sister Thérèse was a woman in her late twenties. The first thing he noticed about her was the color of her eyes, so pale they seemed contradictorily intense against the deep black of her habit. Her French was extremely rapid.

"Monsieur Lédard," she said, "I dislike bothering you, I know you are a busy man. But our problems are exceptional, and perhaps you can help."

Behind her, the secretary eased the door shut.

"Yes, Sister, what assistance do you need?" he asked. He was already wondering whether there indeed existed a problem of walls needing to be buttressed, or whether this was simply another bid for charity. Sister Thérèse glanced once at the closed door behind her, and then turned to face him again. She reached into the sleeve of her habit, and a pistol suddenly appeared in her right hand. It was a Luger, he knew the weapon well from his days in the Army. But he had never before seen one with a silencer on its muzzle.

In German now, she said, "So Herr Saalfeld, are you ready?"

He knew only paralyzing fear. He could not see the

color of her hair beneath the cowl, but he knew for certain that she was the blond woman about whom he had been warned.

"Nothing to say?" she asked in German.

"I . . ." He shook his head. His throat was constricted, he could not move words past his lips. Belatedly, his hand reached out for the intercom button on his desk, and then jerked back spasmodically when the bullet entered his head. She moved swiftly to the desk. He was slumped in the leather chair, his eyes open and staring. She put the silenced muzzle of the gun close to his temple, whispered, "*Auf Wiedersehen, Herr Saalfeld*," and squeezed the trigger again.

In a little while, she left the office. To the secretary outside, she said in French, "Thank you so much, he is a good, kind man."

Cologne, Germany: April 22, 1974

All day yesterday, he had waited for Karin's call, and finally had phoned the *Meurice* at three P.M., only to learn that she'd checked out early in the morning. He could not understand. The call from Marguerite Deveaux came not ten minutes later. He snatched the receiver from its cradle, thinking it might be Karin. He learned then that Rudolph Saalfeld had been murdered in Lagny that morning, by a woman masquerading as a nun.

Now, not twenty hours later, he waited in the house on *Freiherr-Vom-Stein-Strasse* for Johanna's return, knowing she would bring with her information on Koenig's woman in Belsen. His mind was not on Koenig's woman; he could not stop thinking of Karin Phillips. He told himself she had left Paris without phoning only because it had been simpler that way, swifter, less cruel. They had spent a romantic evening together, and she had made extravagant predictions, but in the pale Parisian light of an April dawn, she had reconsidered, and made her decision, and acted upon it immediately. He told himself she had left the *Meurice* at nine A.M. only to avoid a painful confrontation. But he knew that Rudolph Saalfeld had been slain at ten o'clock, and he knew his murderer had been a woman. And a blonde had been following Rausch in Berlin. And Karin Phillips was a blonde who had never been to Berlin, but who knew about the Charlottenburg *schloss*.

Johanna came into the house at close to midnight. She looked extremely tired. She poured herself some *Kirschwassar*, and then took her notes from her handbag.

"This can wait till morning, if you prefer," Michael said.

"No, it can't," she said. "You are to meet with Edstrand at ten-thirty. You had best know all this."

"How much did they find out?" he asked.

"Enough. There *was* a woman in Belsen. Her name was Kristin Grosse. She died in childbirth in October of 1945."

"Koenig's child?" Michael asked.

"Yes. A daughter."

"And *her* name?"

"Lisa Beck."

"Beck? Is she married now?"

"No. That is her maiden name. She was raised by an aunt and uncle in America. They adopted her."

"Where in America?"

"Minnesota. You are getting ahead of me, Michael."

"Sorry."

"Edstrand sent a very good man to Belsen, he talked to the child's grandfather. The grandmother died in 1951, when the child was six. That was when she was sent to America. The grandfather felt he could not raise her alone. He was not, by the way, either a baker *or* a pastry chef."

"What was he?"

"*Ein Wurstfabrikant*. A sausage maker."

"Lisa Beck," Michael said. "October, 1945. That would make her . . ."

"Almost twenty-nine years old."

"Yes," he said, and fell silent.

"Does that mean anything?" Johanna asked.

"No, no. Besides, if she's in Minnesota . . ."

"No, Michael. She is not in Minnesota. She is here. In Germany."

"How do you know that?"

"She wrote to her grandfather in February. She said she was coming to Germany in March, to find her true father. She mentioned him by name in the letter. She wrote '*mein richtiger Vater, Ernst Koenig.*' As soon as we received this information, Edstrand checked with Customs and Immigration. She is here, no question. She arrived on March first."

"Where did she come in?"

"Frankfurt."

"On March first. A month before Stolz was killed."

"Precisely."

"Where is she now?"

"We have no idea."

"While Edstrand was checking passports, why didn't he . . . ?"

"He did. In March, there was no record for a Lisa Beck at any hotel in Frankfurt. And there is no record of her now, either. Not any place in Germany."

"Another passport?"

"It would have to be."

"What does she look like?" Michael asked.

"Her grandfather only had pictures of her as a child. She was extraordinarily beautiful. Blonde, with light eyes."

"Light? Does that mean blue or green?"

"The photographs were in black and white. There was no way of . . ."

"Well, didn't he *ask*? What the hell kind of agent did Edstrand send?"

"Why is this upsetting you so, Michael?"

"I hate sloppy work," he said. "If a man's sent to do a job, then let him do the damn thing right!"

"He did a very thorough job," Johanna said flatly. "I'm tired. I think I'll go to bed."

"Was there anything else in the report?"

"Nothing."

"Do they know whether she made contact with her father?"

"I have told you everything that was in the report."

"Where do I meet Edstrand tomorrow?"

"In the gardens. As usual."

"*That's* getting sloppy, too," Michael said.

"Good night, Michael," Johanna said. "I will talk to you in the morning. Perhaps you'll be feeling better by then."

"I'm feeling fine right now," he said.

"Yes, I see that. Did you plug in Lukas's vaporizer, as I asked?"

"I plugged it in."

"Good night then, Michael," she said, and went out of the living room and into her bedroom. In a little while, he put out all the lights, and went into his own bedroom at the opposite end of the hall.

Cologne, Germany: April 23, 1974

"We will continue, of course," Edstrand said.

"How?" Michael asked. "The only hope we *ever* had of finding Koenig . . ."

"Yes, yes, I realize. But the strategy *was* correct, you must admit that. He *did* finally move against the three of them. It is unfortunate that we lost our bait, the task will be more difficult now . . ."

"They were *people*," Michael said.

"Eh?"

"You talk about them as though they were only pieces of cheese in a trap."

"I do not grieve their loss," Edstrand said flatly, "except as it affects our ability to capture Koenig and bring him to trial."

"And how do you propose to do that?" Michael said. "The three of them are dead. Wherever Koenig's been hiding all these years, he can relax now. His daughter tied up all the loose ends for him."

"Yes. But if she is still in Europe . . ."

"Just try to find her," Michael said. "She's got to have at *least* two passports, and maybe more. She can dye her hair red or black or purple, and leave whenever she chooses."

"In which case we will find her in Minnesota."

"*If* she goes back to Minnesota. Would *you* go back to Minnesota?"

"I do not even know where Minnesota *is*," Edstrand said dryly. "I'm not sure I understand you. What are you suggesting? That we close the file? That would be impossible. There has already been too much time expended."

"*And* money," Michael said sourly.

"Yes, money," Edstrand said.

"Where are we supposed to start?" Michael asked. "That's all I want to know."

"We are now considering our next move. You will be informed."

"What do I do meantime?"

"Take a small holiday. Go fishing. Relax."

"I've forgotten how to relax," Michael said, and

there was such a note of sadness in his voice that Edstrand turned to him where they were sitting on the bench and studied his face soberly, but only for an instant. The empathy lasted no longer that that. Edstrand rose. "There are worse jobs," he said. "We will contact you."

Paris, France: April 23, 1974

That night in Paris, Marguerite Deveaux dined alone, and then went to see a movie afterwards. The movie was about young love. She wept openly when the lovers were separated, and wept again when at last they were reunited at the end of the film. She dried her eyes, and tucked her soggy handkerchief back into her handbag before the theater lights came up. In the handbag, alongside the handkerchief, there was an Astra Falcon, a Spanish-made .380 caliber pistol.

The night outside was pleasant and mild, and she savored the long-overdue balminess of spring as she walked the three city streets to her apartment on the *Rue St. Sulpice*. She found herself out of breath more and more often these days, she would have to pay closer attention to her weight, her doctor had warned her about it. But living alone as she did, she was often tempted to nibble, and whereas she had at least a dozen friends in Paris, none of them really cared enough to chide her about her penchant for sweets. She let herself into the downstairs foyer with her key, turned on the light, closed and locked the entrance door behind her, and then climbed to the first floor, hoping the timer switch would not snap out the bulb before she reached the landing. It did, of course, she moved far too slowly these days, she really would have to see about her diet. She found the first floor switch in the dark, turned on the light ahead and above her, and climbed as quickly as she could to the second floor. Her apartment was close to the stairwell, and she managed to insert her key into the lock before the light went off again. Once inside the apartment, she turned on the overhead kitchen light, and then closed and locked the door behind her. Sighing, she took off her topcoat and hung it behind a flowered curtain near the refrigerator. The apartment was still. She unlaced her low-heeled walking shoes, put them on the floor of the closet, and pulled the flowered curtain closed again. There were reports to finish, she had best do those before morning.

She felt, she realized, an inordinate sense of gloom, the aftermath of Saalfeld's murder. To her, Ernst Koenig was a personal antagonist, an invisible wraith who symbolized all the terrors of the Nazi occupation. Her fiancé had been killed by the Nazis in the summer of 1943, shot to death in the square in the village of La Coquille, a hostage who refused to tell the names of the underground workers who had dynamited a munitions dump two nights before. She would never forget that stifling August afternoon, the flies buzzing in the square, the rifle shots cracking into the stillness. The sunlight splintered like broken glass as he collapsed to the cobblestones, and the

German commandant walked to him, and casually drew his pistol, and delivered the *coup de grâce*. She had not screamed. A scream, a sob, even a tear might have betrayed her and the others in the movement. But that night, alone in the basement room she shared with eight men and two other women, she wept alone on a blanket in the corner and in the morning went back to the village square and looked at the cobblestones that had been hosed clean, and heard the laughter of two German soldiers patroling the streets, and made a silent hateful vow.

She had been seventeen years old on that afternoon in August; she was now forty-eight. Forty-eight. And she wept at movies depicting young love, and she carried in her handbag a Spanish-made pistol which she'd used on more than one occasion. She felt she had lived a dedicated and worthwhile life, she did not consider herself a lonely woman. And yet, before she began writing up the reports, she went to the refrigerator and took from one of the shelves a box of chocolates, which she carried with her into the bedroom. The files were carefully hidden in a fake kerosene heater that rested on the floor below the single window in the bedroom. She unscrewed the four nuts at the back of the heater, and removed from one of the metal shelves a manila folder containing the preliminary notes she had made on the Saalfeld murder. There was a small table opposite the bed. She turned on the light there, put the folder on the table top, and then went back to the bed, to pick up the box of chocolates she had temporarily put down.

As she leafed through the notes, she lifted the lid on the box of chocolates, and idly and indiscriminately selected first one and then another. She continued reading her small precise handwriting; in the *lycée*, she had won a prize for penmanship. Twenty minutes later, she had edited her notes, and was ready to type them. She had eaten a half-dozen chocolates by then, and was reaching for another when a strange feeling of impending calamity overwhelmed her. She had never felt this way in her life, as though doom were imminent, an odd *malaise* that caused her to shudder. And then there was a sense of tightness across her chest, and a sudden stiffness of the neck. *Strychnine*, she thought at once, and in the next instant fell in spasm to the floor. The first convulsion lasted no longer than two minutes. Coming out of it, her pulse weak, her pupils dilated, she crawled to the telephone, only to discover that the wire had been cut. The same overwhelming sense of premonition struck her again. The sudden bleat of a taxicab horn on the street outside precipitated the next paroxysm.

An hour later, she was dead.

Her face was blue, there was a sardonic grin on her lips.

Bonn, Germany: April 24, 1974

He had scarcely known Marguerite, and yet he felt her loss keenly, as though he had received news of the death of a beloved aunt he had known only briefly in his youth. The letter he wrote to the man who was replacing her in Paris read simply, "We regret to learn of your recent loss of personnel, but assure you nonetheless of our continued cooperation." He wanted to add more, but could think of nothing to say. He folded the letter, sealed it in the envelope, and put a stamp on it. In the reception room outside, Mathilde was smacking gum like an American, and carefully watching the clock. It was four-thirty P.M. He told her they both might just as well go home, and was surprised when she took this as a rebuke.

"I have finished already the correspondence," she said in her heavily accented English, and then quickly put the cover on her typewriter, before he could change his mind. As soon as she was gone, he called home to tell Johanna he was on the way, and then locked the front door of Bellis Exports, and took the elevator down to the street level.

Karin Phillips was waiting for him outside the building.

"Small world," she said, and smiled.

She was without her camera this time. She wore a dark blue suit, a white blouse open at the throat, a knotted string of pearls hanging in the open "V" of the suit jacket. Her blond hair was brushed away from her face and knotted severely at the back of her head, emphasizing the finely sculpted nose and good bones. He wanted nothing more than to take her in his arms and hold her close.

"Small world indeed," he said, but the exchange

had worn thin. He looked into her eyes, and tried to read them. Was she a schoolteacher from Brighton, Massachusetts, or was she the daughter of Captain Ernst Koenig? Was she Karin Phillips or Lisa Beck? Whoever she was, she was dangerous. If Karin, he had been on the verge of loving her more completely than any woman he had ever known—and she had disappeared. If Lisa, she was capable of destroying him as effectively as she had destroyed the others.

"I'm here to explain," she said. "Will you buy me a drink?"

She did not wait for his answer. She looped her hand through his arm, and together they began walking up the *Adenauer Allee*. He was aware of her scent, aware of the slight pressure of her breast against his arm. And aware, too, that she was possibly a woman who had committed four murders. Walking silently beside her, waiting for her to explain as she had promised—*but, ah, she had promised in Paris, too, hadn't she*?—he wished desperately that he was wrong. On the night Johanna had reported to him on Lisa Beck, he had been unable to sleep. The connection had seemed apparent to him—there *were* no coincidences in this business. And the next morning, he had withheld from Edstrand any information about the American schoolteacher who only *might* have been in Berlin when Rausch was killed. She was here in Bonn now, and she had told him she was here to explain. So perhaps there was an explanation, after all. He hoped there was a good and valid one. If not . . .

He did not know what.

It wasn't yet five when they reached the bar; the place was almost empty. They found a table away from the jukebox, and Karin ordered a glass of vermouth. He ordered a double scotch on the rocks. They said nothing to each other until the drinks came. Then she raised her glass and said, "Mars stands for sorrow. Peace brings joy and a happy morrow."

He nodded and said nothing.

"So." She sipped at the vermouth and then put the glass on the table. "I'm a terrible coward, forgive me," she said. "This is the most difficult thing I've ever had to do in my life."

"I'm waiting," he said.

"Paris," she said. "I suppose we should begin with Paris."

"That's as good a place as any."

"Well, it's really quite simple," she said. "You see, I fell in love with you, Michael."

"Ah," he said. "That explains everything. That explains why you left early the next morning, it explains why you didn't call . . ."

"Would you like to know when I fell in love with you?"

"Where'd you go when you left Paris, Karin?"

"Why is that important to you?"

"It is."

"I rented a car and drove through the Loire Valley."

"You didn't happen to pass through Lagny, did you?"

"Lagny. No." She shook her head. "Where's Lagny?"

"You left Paris on the morning of the twenty-first, and you went on a trip through the Loire Valley . . ."

"Yes."

"And then what did you do?"

"I returned to Paris."

"When?"

"On the twenty-third."

"Were you in Paris last night?"

"Yes. Michael, why are you throwing all these dates at me?"

"The dates are meaningful."

"In what way?"

He had come too far; there was no place to go but to accuse her. Rudolph Saalfeld had been killed on the twenty-first, Marguerite Deveaux last night. He would either have to question her about the murders without innuendo or indirection, or else retreat. He settled for the partial truth.

"I'm simply trying to find out who you are," he said.

"You know who I am."

"Do I?"

"Perhaps not," she said, and lifted her glass again, and this time swallowed a large gulp of vermouth. "Never mind," she said, "forget it. I was an idiot to come here. I should have gone to London, I should have followed my damn itinerary."

"Why *didn't* you go to London?" he asked.

"Because I wanted to tell you I love you. I thought it was terribly important to tell you exactly *when* I fell in love with you, and how I . . ."

"And when was that?" he asked.

"The hell with it," she said.

"I want to know."

"It was when you admitted you were frightened. I've known too many men who'd never admit to being frightened about anything. I always had the feeling they were trembling inside." She lowered her eyes. "I don't believe that about you, Michael. I think you're very brave and very strong, and also very frightened. And I love you for it."

"Why did you leave Paris without calling me?" he asked.

"Because I had to make the most important decision in my life." She looked up at him. "I had to make it alone. That's why I drove through the Loire Valley, and wandered through all those dark, clammy castles . . ."

"And have you made the decision?"

"I'm here," she said simply.

"I'm still not sure what that means. Your being here."

"It means I've decided not to go back. I'm staying in Europe, Michael, I'm making the break. And, if you want me . . ."

"I want you," he said.

Assmannshausen, Germany: April 24, 1974

It was less than a two-hour drive from Bonn to Bingen, on the left bank of the Rhine, but they hit heavy traffic outside Koblenz, and then drove the next sixty kilometers leisurely, enjoying the glorious countryside at twilight. They arrived in Bingen at close to eight o'clock. They walked hand in hand through the small port, and he explained to her that the Rhine changed direction at this spot, cutting northward abruptly, cutting through the *Bingen Loch*, which narrow passage was treated with extreme respect by navigators. He pointed out the *Mäuseturm*, the "Mouse Tower" guarding the entrance to the passage, and told her how it had got its name.

"There was once an archbishop named Hatto . . ."

"In days of yore," she said. "You forgot 'In days of yore.' "

"Yes, in days of yore," he repeated, and smiled, and squeezed her hand. "He was the archbishop of Mainz, and there was a particularly hard winter one year, and the people were starving, and they came to him for relief. Well, he rounded up all the beggars he could find, and locked them in a barn, and set fire to it. And while the barn was burning, he giggled and said, 'Listen to my mice squeaking.' "

"How *awful*!" Karin said.

"Ah yes, but a great army of mice ran out of the barn and chased him all the way to the Bingen Tower, and ate him."

"That's even *more* awful," she said.

"Hence the *Mäuseturm*," he said.

"You're not a very interesting guide," she said, "but you're terribly attractive."

"I love you, too," he answered.

They took the car ferry across the Rhine, and then drove northward on the right bank to *Assmannshausen*, and booked a room in a sixteenth century inn where Goethe once had stayed. The chef, they were told, was originally from Frankfurt, and he had prepared for the menu that night a specialty of his native city, a sweet and sour eel soup called *Aalsuppe*. He suggested, too, that they try either the *Schweinekamm*, a roasted salt pork, or the *Schweinekotlett*, a breaded pork chop. Pork, he explained, was a specialty of the Hesse region, though of course the venison was delicious as well, and the Rhine salmon was without peer. If madam preferred chicken, however, he could highly recommend the *Bremer Kükenragout*, which was prepared in a thick cream sauce of vegetables. Karin decided not to risk the eel soup; to start, she ordered a *Zweibelkuchen*, a flat pasty filled with onions, and then immediately said, "You won't want to kiss me afterwards."

"I'd want to kiss you even if you ordered onions flavored with garlic," he said.

They were both famished, and neither spoke for at least the first five minutes of the meal, Michael eating the soup with thick slices of butter-spread pumpernickel, Karin devouring the onion pasty. They looked up suddenly, as though realizing at the same moment how absolutely piggish they'd been, and just as suddenly burst into laughter. Michael poured more Reisling, and they ate the rest of the meal more leisurely, and talked without interruption, as though anxious now to make up for their earlier gluttonous silence. After dinner, they walked along the river, and listened to the bells in a distant church tower. It was past eleven when they went up to the room.

He had not yet told her about Johanna. Nor had he called Cologne to say he would not be home that night. He could not call from the telephone in the room. Or could he? He hesitated. Should he tell Karin the truth? He decided against it, said he wanted to go down to the car park to check on whether he had locked the car, and then phoned Johanna from the lobby. She asked immediately where he was, and he told her he was in Assmannshausen. She said she had been worried about him, and was glad to hear he was all right. He asked how Lukas's cold was, and she said he seemed to be feeling better.

"Well, good night then," he said.

"Good night, Michael."

Gently, he put the receiver back on its cradle, and then went upstairs to where Karin was waiting.

In the morning, when he awoke, she was gone.

He looked at his watch. It was only nine-thirty, he thought at first that she had awakened early and gone down to breakfast without him. But the clerk at the desk told him that madam had come down at dawn and requested a taxi to Cologne. Teutonically polite, only his raised eyebrows expressed the suspicion that perhaps they had quarreled. Michael thanked him, paid the bill, and left the hotel.

Cologne, Germany: April 25, 1974

Viktor Edstrand was a man who disliked puzzles of any kind.

It was perhaps for this reason that he had entered this idiotic profession many years back. He still chose to call it a profession, though many of its means were amateurish and most of its ends inglorious. Edstrand liked solutions. He did not particularly care for the long and tortured processes that led to the solutions, but he supposed that was all part of the game, as his American colleagues often put it.

The death of Marguerite Deveaux annoyed him.

It did not disturb him, it merely annoyed him. It annoyed him because it introduced into the reasoning process an unexpected development that made resolution more difficult. He saw the sequence of events rather like an interminable tragedy in five acts. The star of this inept little melodrama was Ernst Koenig, but he never appeared on stage, and the audience had long ago forgotten who he was or what he'd done. In his place, they were introduced to a daughter, Lisa Beck. Besides being unquestionably beautiful, she was superbly talented besides, capable of firing a Luger pistol with deadly accuracy, or constructing a homemade bomb, or injecting chocolates with enough strychnine to fell a horse. A remarkable actress indeed, fluent in English, which she had learned from her adoptive parents in Minnesota; *and* French, which she had spoken when disguised as a nun in Lagny; *and* German, which she had learned as a child in Belsen. The hapless character actors in this morality play were three of the victims—Stolz, Rausch, and Saalfeld. The fourth victim, Marguerite Deveaux should have served no greater purpose than to introduce a scene or two, answer the telephone, announce that dinner was now being served on the terrace. And yet, she had unknowingly ingested more than fourteen grams of strychnine; someone most assuredly had wanted her dead. Edstrand saw himself as the *raisonneur* in this bleak charade, the man entrusted with the thankless task of making sense out of something that now appeared nonsensical. Sitting in his kitchen on the *Ehren Strasse*, he sipped his morning coffee and looked through the window at the rooftops of Cologne. The facts seemed simple and direct, the rising dramatic line conclusive. The only thing lacking was a denouement. He went over the facts again, examining each in turn:

In the city of Frankfurt, on the thirty-first of March, a man named Hans Stolz was shot to death with a Luger pistol. There were no clues as to the identity of his murderer.

In the city of Berlin, on the seventeenth of April, a man named Helmut Rausch was killed when a bomb exploded in his automobile. He had previously stated that he was being followed by a blond woman in a black raincoat.

In the Parisian suburb of Lagny, on the twenty-first of April, a man named Rudolph Saalfeld was shot to death with a Luger pistol. His killer was a woman wearing a nun's habit. A ballistics comparison of bullets and shell casings proved conclusively that the murder weapon was the same one that had killed Hans Stolz in Frankfurt.

Ergo—was it not reasonable to assume that the same woman had killed all three men?

Edstrand sipped at his coffee. On the rooftop opposite his window, he saw a pair of pigeons, one following the other across the orange tiles. He went back to his deductive reasoning:

Lisa Beck was the daughter of Ernst Koenig.

She had been described as a blonde.

She had come to Europe in search of her father.

She had most certainly entered the country through Frankfurt, on the first day of March.

She had since vanished from sight.

Ergo—was it not equally reasonable to assume that Lisa Beck had indeed found her father, and had then proceeded at his behest to eliminate the three men who had betrayed his secret? Yes, Edstrand thought, it is possible. It is not only possible, it is also quite probable and in fact highly likely.

Why then, he wondered, had Lisa Beck *also* killed Marguerite Deveaux?

On the rooftop opposite, the female pigeon waddled away over the tiles, and the male immediately followed. The eternal game, he thought. The hunter and the quarry, the pursuer and the pursued. But much more deadly when it did not involve romance.

Or was the death of Marguerite Deveaux entirely unrelated to the Koenig investigation? She had, after all, been involved in other projects; as was the case with most of their agents, Daisy had not been her sole assignment. So perhaps her death was merely a coincidence, an accident of timing that only made it *seem* related to Daisy. No, there were no coincidences in this business. He intuitively sensed and believed without question that Marguerite had been killed because she had been one of the agents assigned to Daisy. In which case, *any* of the agents assigned to Daisy . . .

Something had startled the pigeons on the roof opposite. He looked up as they took sudden flight into the sky. And then, from the corner of his eye, he saw the glint of sunshine on metal. He tried to throw himself away from the window and the table, but he was an instant too late. The glass shattered inward, its shards covering the breakfast dishes and his unfinished cup of coffee. On his back on the floor, he gasped for breath, and then all breathing stopped, and his hands twitched for seconds only and were still.

Cologne, Germany: April 26, 1974

"My son is involved," Johanna said.

"I care about Lukas as much as you do," Michael replied.

"Perhaps. But he is not your son. Edstrand was *killed* yesterday, do you know what that means?"

"I think I do."

"It means we are all in danger," Johanna said. "Any of us who have ever had anything to do with Daisy are now in danger of being killed. Any of us, *all* of us. And that's why I'm afraid for Lukas."

"I don't think she'll move against Lukas," Michael said.

"How can you be sure of that? We are not dealing with a rational person here, Michael. This is no longer polite espionage, passwords and counter passwords, the whole secret nonsense of . . ." She hesitated. Emboldened by the look of sudden understanding on his face, she said, "Yes, that is what I think it is. Nonsense. I have thought so for a long time. I have thought it is nonsense, and I have thought we are fools. To live like this, depriving ourselves of normal lives, to live instead this *sham*. Yes, Michael, nonsense. I am weary of our governments, Michael. My husband was killed serving his precious government, and I do not wish his son to be killed now, only because *I* am also serving that same government. For what, Michael? I will tell you something. My son is more important to me than my government."

"What do you want to do, Johanna?"

"I want to leave. She is here in Cologne. If she knew where to find Edstrand, she knows where to find us as well."

"Then leave," he said.

"What will they do to me?" she asked.

"They won't do anything to you."

"Won't they? There are no differences in methods, Michael. Only in ideologies. I may have as much to fear from our own people as from Lisa Beck."

"They can't fault you for leaving. If there's even the possibility that Lukas may be harmed . . ."

"Defection, it is called," she said dryly.

"Survival, it is called," he answered. "Where will you go?"

"I'm not sure yet. Out of Cologne. Maybe even out of Germany. I don't know." She hesitated. "Will you come with us?"

"No," he said. "I want her to find me."

"Why? Do you care so much? Do you *really* care so much about Ernst Koenig?"

"I care about *her*. She killed five people. I want her to find me."

"She will kill you, too, Michael. You are a fool."

He did not answer. She stared at him for a moment, searching his face, and then she put her hand gently on his arm.

"Michael, come with us," she said.

"Go, Johanna," he said. "And be careful." This was the closest they had come to sharing an honest emotion in the three years they had known each other. "Please, *please* be careful," he said, and turned away quickly.

He wanted her to gain easy access to the house, and he had not locked any of the doors when Johanna and the boy departed. He sat in the living room now, a single light burning behind him, the ticking of the grandfather clock the only sound in the house. A copy of the German magazine *Der Stern* was folded open on his lap. His hand was under the magazine, and in his hand there was a Smith & Wesson .32 caliber revolver. The clock read nine thirty-five. He had not expected her to come for him before nightfall, but it had been dark for several hours now. Well, perhaps she would try in the morning. She seemed to have no aversion for murder in the daylight, this demented daughter of an officer of the Third Reich. Perhaps, when Michael next drove to Bonn, and unlocked the front door of Bellis Exports, a pail of acid would fall upon his head. Or the floor would cave in beneath him. Or the walls would suddenly grow iron spikes and close in upon him. Or the room would fill with water, drowning him. He remembered what Saalfeld had said to him in Paris: "*If a man forgets how to smile, he also forgets how to live.*" Michael could find very little to smile about tonight. He was waiting for Lisa Beck, or, as she preferred to call herself, Karin Phillips.

At ten minutes to ten, he heard the back door opening.

He did not move.

He heard her footsteps in the kitchen, and then in the corridor outside the living room, and still he did not move.

She came into the living room. She was unarmed, or at least she showed no weapon; she was, however, wearing a bag slung from her shoulder. Under the magazine, his finger slid inside the trigger guard of the .32.

"Good evening, Michael," she said.

"Good evening, Karin," he answered.

"I'd like you to come with me," she said.

The gun in his lap was pointed at her middle. The action was hair-trigger. His finger hovered over the curved steel.

"We can do what we have to do right here, Fräulein Beck," he said, and with his left hand removed the magazine from his lap, revealing the pistol.

She looked at the gun. "Ah," she said.

"Ah," he repeated. "Throw your bag to me."

"This is ridiculous," she said, but she unslung the bag and tossed it to where he was sitting. With his left hand, he went through it. The hand holding the gun was still leveled at her midsection. On top of the clutter in the bag, he found a Browning automatic.

"No Luger?" he said. "I'm surprised."

"I'm not Lisa Beck," she said.

"Then how do you know what I mean?"

"What?"

"The reference to the Luger. If you're not Lisa Beck . . ."

"I know as much about her as you do. Perhaps more. Michael, we're wasting time here . . ."

"Shut up," he said. There was an American passport in the bag. He opened it to the page opposite her picture. The name in the passport was Karin Phillips. Her home address was given as Commonwealth Terrace, Brighton, Massachusetts. The passport didn't mean a thing; his own passport identified him as Michael Henderson. He put the passport back into the bag, and then slipped the Browning into his jacket pocket.

"Who are you?" he said. "You don't expect me to believe that phony passport, do you?"

"Of course not."

"What *is* your name?"

"I can't tell you that."

"Why not?"

"For the same reason you can't tell me yours. We're in the same business, Michael."

"I don't believe you."

"*Believe* me, please."

"Why'd you leave Paris the day you promised to call me?"

"Because I had instructions to cover Saalfeld in Lagny sur Marne."

"Then you *didn't* go on a trip through the Loire Valley."

"No, I didn't."

"Were you in Paris the night Marguerite Deveaux was killed?"

"Yes. Michael, we've been minutes late each time.

We receive new information, we act upon it, and she's already been there and gone."

"Who's *we*?" he asked.

"Our cell. I know *your* people work in cells, too; I have photographs of everyone in your cell."

"Is that why you took my picture in the park that day?"

"Yes. To identify you and the others to our own agents. We did not want any mistakes. Michael, don't you see? We're working for the same cause, we have the same job . . . finding Ernst Koenig and bringing him to trial for murder. At least, that *was* our job. It now includes finding Lisa Beck as well."

"Who are you working for? Israel?"

"Don't ask me questions you know I can't answer."

"But you're not American."

"No, I'm not American."

"Why'd you come here tonight?"

"To get you out of here. She won't try for you here, Michael, she's too smart for that. There are too many other houses in the area, she can't be sure of who's in them."

"Where do you want to take me?"

"Someplace more secluded. Where we can get her if she tries."

"I'm to be the bait, is that it?"

"I love you too much to put your life in danger, Michael. You'll be well protected."

"Say it again."

"Say . . . ?"

"That you love me too much."

"Ah, Michael, I love you *much* too much. But it's hopeless, don't you agree?"

"Why?"

"Because you're married."

"I'm not married."

"Please, I know about your wife, I know about Johanna. I've known from the beginning."

"She's not my wife."

"Michael, I had it checked. The marriage certificate is filed right here in Cologne. Please don't lie to me, I've agonized over this far too much already."

"I'm not married," Michael said, "I've never *been* married. Johanna isn't my wife, the marriage was our cover here in Cologne. False names, false marriage certificate, false everything. We've never so much as held hands in the past three years. She's not my wife, believe me."

"If only I could," Karin said. "I was telling you the truth when I said I was ready to make the most important decision in my life. But I wasn't talking about teaching, Michael, I was talking about espionage. I want to get out, I *will* get out once Koenig is found. But . . . I wanted to get out with *you*. I wanted to spend the rest of my life with you."

"Then believe me," he said.

They moved toward each other tentatively, each afraid to believe, each conditioned not to believe. He lowered the pistol. As he took her into his arms, he realized he didn't even know her name, and as he kissed her he thought only that he wanted to tell her at once who he was, tell her all there was to know about him, reconstruct for her a past that had vanished in a maze of false identities in far too many cities. Still clinging to each other, their eyes searching, they heard a voice behind them say, in English, "That's very nice. Don't move." Startled, they broke apart.

The woman standing in the doorway was a tall blonde wearing a black raincoat. There was a Luger in her hand, and a silencer was on its muzzle.

"Throw the gun on the floor," she said.

The Luger was trained on Karin, he had no choice but to throw his own pistol onto the rug. The woman stooped, picked it up, and put it in a pocket of the raincoat.

"Anything you'd like to say?" she asked. "Say it quickly."

There was nothing to say, he knew that. He had been trained to accept the inevitability of one day facing a loaded pistol held by a man or a woman with pale murderous eyes. There was nothing to say, but he tried nonetheless.

"Are you Lisa Beck?" he asked.

"Yes," she said. "I'm Lisa Beck."

The Browning he had taken from Karin's shoulder bag was in the left-hand pocket of his jacket. He dared not make a move for it. And yet, he had to move soon—or not at all.

"You were foolish to come here," he said. "The neighboring houses . . ."

"I've been watching them since dusk," she said. "I

have nothing to fear from the good German burghers living on this street."

His left hand moved tentatively toward the pocket, but her eyes were still on him. He wiped the palm of his hand on the fabric instead, hoping she would accept it as a nervous reaction. His hand dropped to his side again. "Lisa," he said, "they'll get your father, anyway. Whether you kill us or not, they'll get him sooner or later."

"No," she answered, and smiled bleakly. "They've *already* got him, Mr. Henderson. My father is dead. He died in Frankfurt the week after I found him. He was living there under the name of the man whose identity he'd stolen all those years ago. Sick and old . . . he looked eighty-five, he was only fifty-six. Afraid to go outdoors, afraid they'd find him. Afraid you or one of the others would find him. I watched him die. I'd come to Europe only hoping to locate the father I'd never known, and I found him, and watched him die—and knew who had killed him."

"He killed himself," Michael said. "He killed himself the day he robbed another man of his life and his identity."

"No!" Lisa said angrily. "He was hounded to death. He was a sick old man living in fear of his life, and when finally he died, I knew what had to be done next. He'd told me the names of his accusers, but I didn't know where they were, nor was I an experienced assassin. I had to learn. I had to find people who would forge passports, and show me how to assemble a bomb, I had to learn about poisons and pistols, I had to learn. I learned well," she said, and smiled again. The smile this time contained enormous satisfaction and something more frightening than anything Michael had ever seen on the face of a human being before. It contained finality. In a moment, she would squeeze the trigger.

"Your father killed a man," Karin said.

She turned toward Karin sharply, her eyes blazing. In that instant, Michael thrust his left hand into the pocket of his jacket, and groped for the butt of the unfamiliar pistol.

"Yes!" Lisa said. "He killed a man, *yes*! And *you* killed him in turn. You and the three fools who told about him at the . . ."

He fired through the pocket. The bullet ripped through the fabric of his jacket, and through the fabric of the black raincoat and through the body of the woman who had come there to kill them. Deflected, it struck the grandfather clock behind her, and shattered the dial, and he could think only that the clock was the one thing Johanna had loved about this house. The acrid stench of cordite filled the room. He felt suddenly sick to his stomach.

Karin went to him, and gently lifted her hands to his face, and very softly said, "It's finished now."

And he said, "Yes, it's finished," and did not know whether she understood the larger meaning of his words. For him, it was finished. Michael Henderson had died with Lisa Beck. It was time to go home; he had been away too long.

In a little while, he would tell her who he was.